This one is for Nana Marie

Author's Note

I've always loved the simplicity of the concept of *Frankenstein*. The idea of a fully formed creature propelled into the world – without any sense of who or what he is – has always fascinated me. With *Stitch*, I wanted to explore this idea for myself. I very deliberately decided Stitch wouldn't have any magical powers, or some grand destiny. If he had a power, I wanted it to be his boundless optimism, his belief in the goodness of people and his innate kindness.

I don't set out to write books "about" things. I prefer to be led by my characters, to find the story first. Stitch led me to write about a hero whose heroism is grounded in his imagination and empathy. I believe that empathy is an imaginative act, and that cruelty is its very opposite. Empathy allows everyone to imagine what it's like to be in someone else's shoes, and I hope that Stitch himself embodies that quality.

Stitch eventually led me to write a book about how, as he puts it, "everyone is different". He led me to write a book about the lack of imagination that leads to prejudice and hate, a book about seeing beyond cruelty and accepting everyone for who they are. He led me to write a book about death and grief, about friendship and loyalty.

I hope readers take to Stitch as much as I did, that they enjoy seeing the world through his eyes – and have an adventure along the way.

Pádraig Kenny

Morning Time
and a Visit with Henry

Stitch wakes up, just as he always has done for the past five hundred and eighty-four days he has been waking up.

Five hundred and eighty-five now, he thinks as he makes a mark with a piece of chalk on the wall by his bed. He says the words "five hundred and eighty-five" to himself because he can count, and saying the words makes the idea of waking up so many times more real – "more understandabubble", as Henry might say.

Every day is the same. He wakes up in his turret room with its grey stone walls and its rickety old bed and the cobwebbed window with the sun creeping through it.

Every day the same, except of course for the First Day. On the First Day he woke up somewhere else in the castle. He had never woken before that day. It was what the Professor called his "Birth Day". The First Day. The most important day of all.

Stitch has been marking his waking days ever since. He's not completely sure why, but he likes to do it. It makes him feel good. Makes him feel like he is part of the world.

Stitch takes a chunk of cheese from a drawer in his bedside locker and heads over to the corner of the room where Brown Mouse's cage is. He kneels down and opens the small door of the cage and holds the cheese out in the palm of his hand. Stitch smiles as Brown Mouse stirs from the straw at the bottom of his cage. He likes the small darting movements he makes, his wriggledness, the way his tiny nose and whiskers twitch.

"Hello, Brown Mouse," Stitch says as Brown Mouse nibbles on the cheese. Animals eat food. Apparently they need it for some reason that Stitch doesn't entirely understand, but he feeds Brown Mouse anyway because it's what the Professor has asked him to do as part of their agreement for Stitch keeping him as a pet.

Stitch tried eating once. He didn't like it. He took a potato and a slice of bread and first bit one, then the other, then rolled them around in his mouth and mashed them together between his teeth. He did this for about half an hour until they were a mushy paste, then he spat the paste out on to the floor. Henry told him that the main requirement for the eating of food was to feel hungry. Never having felt hungry, Stitch felt he was missing the necessary part of the process to see it to its completion.

Stitch watches Brown Mouse finish his cheese, then he closes the cage door. He feels the sudden urge to look in the other corner where the empty cage is – the one with its mouldering straw and its empty bowl. But Stitch doesn't turn his head. He doesn't like to look at the empty cage.

"Five hundred and eighty-five days, imagine that," he says to himself as he stands up.

He doesn't know why he says this. It feels like

he is trying to distract himself from something. His voice is a little too loud.

"Well, that's a lot of days now, truth be told. Five hundred and eighty-five. That's almost as many fingers as I have on my hands."

As if to prove the point to himself, Stitch holds his hands up. One is very definitely smaller than the other. This is his left hand. It has long slim fingers. The other is large, almost bloated in comparison. Its fingers are stubby and fat. Both hands are grey in colour because all of Stitch's skin is grey, not like the Professor's skin. His skin is pink with blotches of red on the cheeks just above his white whiskers.

Stitch says goodbye to Brown Mouse before leaving his room.

He goes down the stone spiral staircase, feeling the cold waft from the mossy walls, noting the dewy sparkle of water on the stones, and the way his breath frosts in the air.

He arrives at the end of the hallway. He waits for a moment and listens.

He hears nothing.

This is good because the hallway must be

kept quiet. He walks along it and reaches the door of the Professor's room. He is tempted to listen, but the Professor has expressly told him that he must not be disturbed under any circumstances. He went to bed with those very specific instructions because he was feeling very tired.

Stitch tiptoes past the Professor's door and descends deeper into the castle.

Down another spiral staircase he goes, down past the vast rooms that house the machinery and the conductors and giant fuses and metal machines with their knobs, bulbs, levers, lights. Down where the air moves freely because the rooms are huge. Rooms that were once filled with the tang of lightning.

Down a wooden staircase now, and into the cramped, dimly lit corridor that leads to Henry's room. Stitch pushes the door open and walks in.

"'Allo, Stitch," says Henry in that funny way he has of rolling the words around in his mouth, making it sound as if he is saying the words slowly when really he isn't.

Henry is in his cage, standing on his tippy toes, and looking out the tiny window...

"How'd you know it was me, Henry?"

Henry turns around. He is a lot taller than Stitch. A lot bulkier too. He wears a moth-eaten brown jacket that barely fits across his huge shoulders. His hands are huge, but both are of equal size, a fact that Stitch is slightly jealous of. Henry's face is grey and rectangular and zigzag lines run across it, much like the lines on Stitch's face. Although Stitch has fewer of these zigzags. The Professor has assured him that his zigzags are "much more elegant and subtle".

Henry has big bushy eyebrows and a mop of black hair and he wears big clompy boots. *Clomp clomp* they go sometimes when he paces the wooden floor of his cage. Henry is strictly forbidden to leave his cage because a while ago he didn't behave, and the Professor believes that the most important thing to do is to behave.

"I knew it was you because who else would it have been?" says Henry.

"It could have been the Professor," says Stitch.

He is immediately sorry he has said this because Henry pushes out his lower lip and then flops down on his bed and frowns. He rests his arms on his legs and looks up at Stitch from under his eyebrows.

"The Professor doesn't come to see me," says Henry sulkily. "The Professor doesn't like me."

For a second Stitch is anxious because it looks like Henry is going to cry, so he says what he always says in these situations.

"You came first, Henry."

Henry's face brightens and he grins with pride. "That's right, Stitch. I came first." He takes in a deep breath, grips the lapels of his jacket and pushes his ample chest out. "Me, Henry Oaf. I came first. Before Stitch. That makes me the most importantest one of us all."

Henry gurgles and laughs. He stomps his feet and starts rocking back and forth with joy.

"Me. Henry. Ah hur hur. That's me! Very important and most valuablest and treasurized and appreciatized by all and sundry for being Henry Oaf, my most bestest self."

Stitch lets Henry carry on for a little while because when he gets like this he finds it hard to pay attention.

Eventually Stitch shouts, "Henry!"

Henry shakes his head and laughs, his hair flapping back and forth as he babbles happily to himself.

"Henry!" Stitch shouts, even louder this time.

Henry gives him a look of puzzlement. "What's up now, Stitch?"

Stitch nods at the window. "What were you doing when I came in?"

Henry jerks his thumb towards the window. "Just looking."

"Just looking at what?"

Henry makes a face, as if he has smelled something rotten.

"The sun."

"Oh," says Stitch, sorry he has said anything now because he knows what's coming next.

"The sun isn't like the moon, Stitch." Henry stands up and adopts what he calls his "pontificatory pose".

"Both are round, right enough, that is to say spheracular in their nature, which is a scientificacious term for their roundness. But the similarifications end there and beyond that the moon is far superior in its qualities of light and heat."

"Henry—"

"For one," says Henry, counting things off on his fingers, "the moon's light is calming and pellucidatory, giving a most pleasing coolness to the eyes that can almost be felt."

"Henry—"

"For two, the moon can be looked at, and to be able to look at something is to be able to appreciate its qualities, of which the moon's qualities are manifold."

"What's *mennyfold*?" asks Stitch.

Henry crosses his arms and looks imperious. "It means having the quality of having lots of things contained within your person."

"Like a bag filled with things?"

Henry strokes his chin and looks wise. "I suppose one could ascertainize that conclusion from the facts one observalizes in the world. When something can be compared to another thing, there is a special word for that."

"Which is?"

 17

Henry looks offended. "I don't know, Stitch. What am I, a dictionary?"

Stitch grins. "You are not that, Henry. Certainly not. You are Henry Oaf."

Henry gives a little flourish and a bow. "Whole and complete in myself."

"Have a good day, Henry."

Stitch turns to go, then sighs when Henry says, "Oi, Stitch."

Henry's face is pressed up against the bars of his cage. He has a pleading look.

"What, Henry?"

"Do you think maybe, perhaps, would indeed it be possible if I were to, y'know...?"

Stitch shakes his head. "I can't let you out, Henry. The Professor said."

"But the Professor is asleep," says Henry in a squeaky little voice while miming sleeping with his hands. "He won't know."

"He will. The Professor always knows."

"Please, Stitch? Just for a mo, a minute, a tiny bit, a teeny particular part of a second. Please."

"But you break things, Henry."

Stitch feels guilty when he sees the look on Henry's face. It is as if he has told him the worst news in the world ever, and that Henry alone is responsible for this news, this calamity. Henry lowers his head. His voice is low and sorrowful.

"All right, Stitch."

Stitch feels bad, but Henry can't be allowed out under any circumstances. These are the Professor's orders, and the Professor knows best. And besides, Henry breaks things.

Stitch leaves Henry's room. He still feels bad for Henry, and to distract himself from feeling this way, he does his chores. He goes through the castle and he polishes and sweeps and he tidies things away.

In the late afternoon he goes outside the castle and looks at the garden. It is a riot of colour and deep greens, and it is always growing. Stitch doesn't know how it does this, all this growing and spreading and getting bigger. It fascinates him.

He goes to the edge of the precipice upon which the castle sits. He can see smoke in the distance, coming from the chimneys in the village below the mountain. He sees tiny specks moving about, and he wonders what it would be like to be down there and up close. What would the people look like, he wonders. Like the Professor, maybe, with his even-sized hands and his pink skin. He's not sure why he thinks they would be like that.

He wonders what lies beyond the mountains and forest. Thinking these things makes him feel light-headed, almost excited.

He stays for a while, well into evening. The sky darkens. The stars come out. The village is now a small constellation of warm lights.

Stitch goes back inside. Henry is already asleep, snoring on his bed with his face buried in his arm. Stitch closes his door quietly and leaves him to his dreams. Stitch tiptoes past the Professor's bedroom so as not to disturb him.

Stitch enters his bedroom and lights a candle. He takes the large book from the table by the window. It is a book Henry gave him called *The Great Book of Exploration*. Stitch can't read, but he likes to look at the sketches of faraway lands, places covered in ice, or smothered in jungle vines, and on his favourite page of all is a sketch of an explorer. He is a large man wearing furs, standing with his hands on his hips looking out across an icy tundra. Stitch often wonders what it would be like to be an explorer, to visit the outside world and its furthest reaches. It is something he would very much like to do.

Stitch closes the book. He stands with his hands on his hips and looks at the wall.

"Five hundred and eighty-five days," he says.

He takes the piece of chalk and reaches under his bed for the rectangular slate almost filled with chalk marks. He counts the marks.

"Three hundred and twenty-six."

Stitch makes another chalk mark.

"Three hundred and twenty-seven," he says.

He puts the slate away, gets into his bed, and blows out the candle.

He lies back and looks at the moon-dappled ceiling.

"Three hundred and twenty-seven," he says again.

The Professor has been asleep for a very long time.

Surprise Guests

BOOM BOOM.

Stitch is woken by the sound that echoes through the castle.

It comes again.

BOOM BOOM.

Stitch wonders what it can be. Then he realizes.

The door. Somebody is at the main door. There is a huge metal knocker in the shape of a dragon's head on the door. Stitch used to knock with it out of curiosity, until one day a very annoyed Professor told him to stop.

BOOM BOOM.

Stitch leaps out of bed. Down the stairs he goes, hurtling around corners, down into the great hallway where the BOOM BOOM sound now clangs and echoes against the stone walls like the clapper against the inside of a great bell.

"Wait now! Wait!" Stitch cries out.

He skids to a halt just before the great oak door, unlocks it, pulls back the latch – and opens the door.

Stitch winces because the door moves with a great creaking sound. A tall man and a young girl are standing on the step outside. Behind them, another man is unloading luggage from a horse-drawn carriage.

Stitch puts a finger to his lips. "Shh, the Professor is asleep and must not be disturbed."

The man looks down on him with a faint smile. He is wearing a long, dark coat with a fur collar, a tall hat, striped trousers and shiny brown shoes. A silver locket hangs from a chain around his neck. His hair is long and stops just above his jawline.

The girl is about Stitch's height. She is wearing a simple floral cream dress decorated with roses and a pair of scuffed black ankle boots.

Stitch has never seen so many people before. They all look so interesting and so different. They are just as he imagined they would be, but also they are not.

They have the same number of hands and legs, and their skin is just like the Professor's, but each one looks different in their own way.

The man sticks his hand out. Stitch looks at it.

"Very pleased to meet you. I'm Professor Giles Hardacre, the Professor's nephew."

Stitch looks at the new Professor's hand. Then looks at his face. Stitch looks at the new Professor's hand again. The new Professor lowers his hand, then smiles in an odd way. It makes Stitch feel strange, as if there is something the new Professor knows that Stitch doesn't.

"And this is my assistant, Alice."

"How do you do?" says Alice.

"How do I do what?" asks Stitch.

Alice looks confused. Professor Hardacre laughs. "Well now," he says.

There is a moment when they all look at each other. Then Professor Hardacre gestures at the hall.

"May we come in?"

Stitch nods. "Of course, but why do you want to come in?"

"We are visiting," says Professor Hardacre. "My uncle and I exchanged letters for a time, but I haven't heard from him recently, so I am here to enquire after his welfare."

"The Professor is very well, thank you very much, Professor Hardacre. He has been resting and has asked not to be disturbed under any circumstances."

While Stitch says all this, Professor Hardacre is examining his face with great concentration. He shakes his head, an amazed look in his eyes.

"I'd read his notes but this is remarkable," he says. "Simply remarkable."

"What is?" asks Stitch.

"Why you are, of course, *you* are," says Professor Hardacre, as if this is the most obvious answer in the world.

Stitch feels confused again. Professor Hardacre brushes past him and takes his gloves off while looking around the great hallway. Alice follows him. She looks at Stitch in what Stitch thinks is a very serious and very direct fashion, then she seems to examine the hallway, before looking at Stitch again. Her gaze makes Stitch feel strange. It's almost as if it compels him to say something, but he doesn't know what to say. Professor Hardacre shouts back over his shoulder. "Mr Vries, if you would be so kind as to carry in our luggage."

The man outside starts to take large trunks and suitcases from the carriage. He turns with a case in each hand and is partway to the door when he suddenly stops and blinks at Stitch. He says a word that Stitch has never heard before.

Mr Vries continues just inside the hall, drops the bags, and then immediately retreats. Stitch smiles at him and waves. Mr Vries can't seem to take his eyes off Stitch. He constantly mutters under his breath. His puffy face reddens as he carries more and more bags in. Eventually he has all the luggage piled just inside the door.

He refuses to move it in any further, and there is a heated discussion between himself and Professor Hardacre about the matter.

"I've been paid to take it this far and no further; nobody said anything to me about stairs," says Mr Vries. All the while he keeps stealing glances at Stitch, occasionally shaking his head as if in disbelief. Stitch smiles at Alice, unsure of what to say.

Eventually Professor Hardacre hands Mr Vries some money. Mr Vries makes a face and waddles away from the door. Stitch watches as he climbs up on to the seat of the carriage. He thrashes the reins hard and heads down the mountain.

"What's your name?" Alice asks Stitch.

Professor Hardacre is still taking in his new surroundings. "I hardly think that is a matter of consequence," he says, without looking at Alice.

"Stitch," replies Stitch.

Professor Hardacre snorts. "How very apt."

Stitch frowns. "What's *apt*?"

"Your name," says Professor Hardacre.

Stitch is confused. "But my name is Stitch. It is certainly not Apt."

But Professor Hardacre isn't listening. He is examining a life-size portrait of the Professor, looking all noble and wise.

"Apt means 'appropriate'. He means your name suits you," says Alice.

Stitch runs a finger along his face. "I suppose it does."

He smiles at Alice. He likes her, even though she doesn't say much. This makes her very unlike

Henry — very unlike anyone he has ever met before — which isn't difficult, because counting the Professor, Henry, the Professor's nephew, Alice herself, Mr Vries and the gentleman from the forest who used to come to the castle at night to leave supplies, he has never really met anyone else before.

Although, the gentleman from the forest was always hooded, and he never saw his face, nor heard him speak anything above a whisper. So perhaps he does not count.

Professor Hardacre speaks, jolting Stitch from his thoughts.

"Well then, shall we meet the old fellow?" he asks.

"What old fellow?" asks Stitch.

"Why my uncle, of course."

"The thing is, the Professor asked not to be—"

But Professor Hardacre is already bounding up the staircase. "I take it his room is where it's always been?" he says.

Stitch and Alice follow him. Up they go, and Stitch has to trot quite quickly to keep up with Professor Hardacre. "Oh, Uncle? Uncle!" Professor Hardacre calls, and Stitch winces once again.

Very soon they are outside the Professor's bedroom. Professor Hardacre places his hand on the doorknob. But Stitch yelps, "Please, Mr Professor's Nephew, the Professor asked very specifically not to be disturbed under any circumstances."

"But this is a special occasion. I'm his favourite nephew," says Professor Hardacre, beaming.

"But he is resting."

"How long has he been resting?"

Stitch has to think for a moment because today hasn't finished. He smiles proudly when he remembers.

"Three hundred and twenty-eight days," he says.

Two things happen at once. Professor Hardacre suddenly turns very pale, and Alice gasps.

Professor Hardacre throws the door open and storms in.

Stitch is taken aback by how violently he does it. He looks at Alice. Alice has a hand clamped to her mouth.

Professor Hardacre stumbles out of the room, wide-eyed, steadying himself against the door frame.

A Strange
and Bewildering Thing

"Dead?" says Stitch.

"Yes," says Alice. "He's gone, Stitch."

Stitch and Alice are sitting at the foot of the great stairs. It is getting dark outside, and for some reason Stitch feels cold, almost as if the darkness has seeped inside him. The rest of the day was spent with Professor Hardacre running about and giving orders. He had Alice move all the luggage to a room upstairs with Stitch's help. Now Stitch is mulling over what Alice has just told him.

"That's what it means," says Alice.

Alice looks at him, searching his face. But she

searches it not in the way Professor Hardacre did. She does it in a kind way.

"So, the Professor is not here any more?" says Stitch.

Alice nods.

"But he will be back?" says Stitch, hopefully.

Alice shakes her head. "No, Stitch. The Professor is gone for ever."

Stitch finds himself thinking about the empty cage again. He does not want to think about the empty cage. If he thinks about the empty cage too long he knows he will start to think about White Rabbit, and thinking about White Rabbit always makes him feel numb and sore at the same time. But if he doesn't think of the empty cage and White Rabbit he thinks about the Professor, and thinking about the Professor makes him feel the same way. He scratches his head agitatedly.

"But if he is gone, where is he gone to?" he asks.

Alice bites her lower lip. "That's a difficult question to answer. But it's best to remember that he is no longer here."

"This is a conundrum and no mistake," he says, his leg bobbing up and down.

Alice stills his leg by gently placing a hand on his knee.

Stitch remembers he has another question for her.

"Do you know many words, Alice?"

"I suppose, yes."

"Have you heard the word *monster*?"

Alice's eyes darken, and she looks grave. "Yes, yes I have."

"Do you know what it means?"

"I do. Where did you hear this word, Stitch?"

"Mr Vries used it earlier. He looked at me and said *monster*. What does it mean?"

Alice sighs. "It's a word some people use to describe others, Stitch. Sometimes the word is apt."

"*Appropriate!*" says Stitch brightly. "I know that word now. It means it suits a thing."

"Well, sometimes the word monster suits a thing, especially if it describes someone or something cruel and horrible. Then that person can be described as a monster. And sometimes someone might use the word to belittle those who look different."

Stitch is bemused by this. "Everyone and everything looks different, Alice. The Professor taught me that. No two things are completely alike. He said..."

Stitch frowns as he tries to remember.

"He said life was *multifarious*. That was the beauty of it, he said."

Stitch grins, but Alice still looks very grave.

"People use some words like weapons, Stitch. They use words to hurt. Take me, for instance. Some people use words to describe me. I've been called a monster too."

Stitch thinks about this. "But if you are a monster, Alice, then that should mean you are horrible and cruel, and I haven't known you for very long, but I know for a fact that you are not horrible and cruel. Far from it. To me you seem to be a very nice individual, wise and generous in your insights and behaviour." Stitch nods to himself. "Very like Henry in some ways, and Henry is my friend, so I think you and I shall be friends too."

He smiles broadly, but Alice turns away from him.

"This is why they call me a monster, Stitch."

There is a silence for a moment while Stitch tries to understand what is going on. Then suddenly he realizes what Alice is saying.

"Because you turn away in the middle of conversations!" he says.

Alice looks befuddled.

"Of course," says Stitch. "Nothing is more horrible and cruel than turning away from someone in the middle of a conversation. Why, sometimes Henry does that to me, and it makes me very cross indeed, although I wouldn't call him a monster. That would be rude…"

"No, Stitch…"

Stitch wags a finger. "Nothing is more terrible than bad manners, I suppose."

"Stitch, no. It's because of this."

She turns away from him again, then turns back to look at him. Stitch is bemused by all of this.

"It's because of my hump. It's because I look different."

Stitch examines her more closely. Indeed, Alice has a hump, for her left shoulder and the top part of her back are larger than the other side, but Stitch paid no mind to that when he first set eyes on her. And he pays no mind to it now, because…

"Everyone looks different, Alice."

She goes to speak, but Stitch holds up his hands.

"It is just a matter of *asymmetry*," he says. "*Asymmetry* is one of the words the Professor taught me. It means there can be parts of things that do not match in terms of shape or size, but then most people, as far as I know, do not correspond in terms of shape or size, so to make a judgement on such a thing..." Stitch snorts. "I mean, that would seem to me to be a most ludicrous idea to have in one's head." Stitch laughs and slaps his leg. "The very idea is comical!"

He laughs again, and then a most peculiar thing happens. He laughs so much that tears spring from his eyes, and those tears become more – what Henry might call "proliferous". Alice looks concerned for him. There are so many tears spilling forth from his eyes, Stitch fears they might keep coming for ever. Everything is a blur now, and all he can think of is the Professor and his face and kind eyes, and Stitch's chest aches.

He has only one question on his mind; it pushes all other thoughts to the side.

"But where is he gone, Alice? Where is the Professor?"

Alice takes his hand in hers and squeezes it. Her hand is warm, not like his hand, which is cold, but there is comfort in it, and the tears eventually stop. Stitch rubs his nose. The strange feeling has passed, although occasionally his shoulders jerk upwards and he makes a sound that is like hiccuping. He suddenly realizes something.

"I will have to tell Henry that the Professor is gone."

"Who is Henry?" asks Alice.

"Henry is my friend. He stays in his cage."

"A cage?"

Alice looks surprised by this information, but before she can say anything else she is interrupted by Professor Hardacre, who is coming down the stairs.

"The poor old fellow. Has been gone for quite some time. Burial arrangements will need to be made." He has some pieces of paper in one hand with words written on them. He sighs and shakes his head, then makes a face. "I may have to notify family members."

Stitch stands up. "Henry must also be notified."

"Henry?" says the new Professor.

"Henry is his friend — who he keeps in a cage," says Alice.

Professor Hardacre appears baffled by this.

Stitch explains who Henry is, and when he does so Professor Hardacre smiles in a very strange way and holds up the papers. "Of course! The other one. My uncle's notes did mention another specimen. I would very much like to meet him."

Introducing Henry

Stitch takes Professor Hardacre and Alice down to Henry's room. Henry is looking out the window and doesn't turn when he hears them come in.

"I do like clouds, Stitch. I think I'm getting to like them more and more. They cover the sun you see. If clouds were people, I think they and I might be friends. What do you think…"

Henry turns and stops mid-sentence as he gapes at the new arrivals.

"This is the Professor's nephew, Henry, and this is his assistant, Alice," says Stitch.

Henry is at a complete loss for words. Stitch has never seen him like this before. He almost looks frightened, and because he looks frightened Stitch feels uncomfortable for some unaccountable reason, as if his stomach is tangled in knots. It is a feeling he does not care for.

"Why is he in a cage?" asks Professor Hardacre. He still has that strange smile.

"Henry breaks things," says Stitch. "He is clumsy, and the Professor said he must stay in the cage until the Professor has decided that he has learned his lesson."

Professor Hardacre advances slowly towards the cage. Stitch notes that Henry takes a little step back, clutching one hand to his chest.

"Hello, Henry," says Professor Hardacre. "I'm very pleased to meet you."

Henry glances at Stitch as if looking for encouragement. Stitch nods at him.

Henry turns to Professor Hardacre. "Well, hello there, Mister Professor's Nephew. I am very pleased to meet you too." He looks at Alice. "And you, Mister Professor's Nephew's assistant Alice."

Alice smiles. "Just Alice will suffice, Henry."

"I have read and heard a great many things about you, Henry," says Professor Hardacre, displaying the papers in his hand.

Stitch notes how Professor Hardacre's words have an immediate effect on Henry. He seems to instantly grow two feet taller.

"Really?" he says. "Although I suppose that is no surprise considering my reputation. The name of Henry Oaf must be known far and wide for many reasons, not least of which are my handsomeness and my innate intellitude, which means I have a grasp of complex things and notions far beyond the minds of those who are not so blessed with such gifts."

Henry puffs his chest out and smiles. Professor Hardacre returns the smile, although Stitch notes it is one that does not seem to find its full expression in his eyes.

"Handsome?" says Professor Hardacre.

"Yes, indeed," says Henry.

"Intelligent?" says Professor Hardacre.

"If that be your preferred pronunciation of the word that best expresses my gifts of deep thought and cleverality."

Henry gives one of his little bows.

Professor Hardacre starts to laugh. Henry's face slackens. Stitch feels bad for him.

"Why, he's almost as amusing as you, Stitch," says Professor Hardacre, still chuckling.

Alice shakes her head in disgust at the Professor's behaviour.

"Let him out," says Professor Hardacre.

"What?" Stitch and Henry say at exactly the same time.

"Let him out," repeats Professor Hardacre.

Stitch fetches the key from the hook on the wall.

"But the Professor..." says a nervous Henry.

"Here's the thing, Henry," says Stitch, and he is just about to tell Henry what has happened to the Professor when Professor Hardacre cuts across him.

"No dilly-dallying, Stitch," says Professor Hardacre, now perusing his notes. He mutters strange words to himself as he reads. Things like "reanimation" and "organic material" and "revivification".

Stitch unlocks Henry's cage. Henry hesitates. Eventually, he shuffles out.

"Well now," he says, looking excited and nervous. "This is a most interesting development."

Professor Hardacre beckons Henry forward without taking his eyes off the notes. "If you would."

Henry moves towards him. The Professor looks up from his notes. His eyes are at chest level with Henry, and he strains to look up into his face. He clicks his fingers impatiently at Alice.

"A stool. Now."

Alice fetches a stool from the corner of the room. Professor Hardacre stands on it. He is now almost at eye level with Henry. He touches Henry's head with one hand, while checking his notes. "Cranial malformation – crude, very crude. Eyes don't match. Clumsy stitching. A certain sloppiness all round, dear Uncle – tsk tsk. I expected better."

Professor Hardacre motions for Henry to turn around and continues to inspect his head. Henry smiles at Stitch, but for some reason Stitch can't seem to smile back. Henry bunches his shoulders and giggles.

"That tickles, Mr Professor's Nephew," he says.

"Hold still," growls Professor Hardacre.

"Ah hur hur," Henry guffaws, and now he starts to rock back and forth and Stitch is worried because this is what usually happens right before Henry goes on one of his more "excitabubble" rampages.

Henry can't seem to take it any longer. His right arm jerks out, hitting Professor Hardacre and sending him flying off the stool. Professor Hardacre hits the ground, his notes spilling around him. Alice runs to him, but he brushes her off and jumps to his feet.

"You fool!" he shouts at a shocked Henry. "I should have known better."

"Should have known better about what, Mr Professor's Nephew?" squeaks a startled Henry.

Professor Hardacre pulls at his waistcoat and runs a hand through his hair. "I mean, look at you. A crude assemblage of odds and ends with no discernible consistency of form. Granted, you resemble a person, in so far as you are a person – which is something I very much doubt can be concluded with any veracity."

"*In so far...?*" says Stitch. He doesn't fully understand them, but something about the words Professor Hardacre has just used makes him feel cold.

The Professor grabs his papers off the floor and consults them again, lost in the words. He seems to have forgotten his fall. Stitch exchanges a glance with Alice, who looks upset and angry.

Henry is twiddling his fingers and swaying back and forth. "Odds and ends?" he says quietly, trying to smile but failing. He looks at Stitch as if seeking comfort, but Stitch doesn't know what to say.

Professor Hardacre continues. "I suppose as an error-strewn first mistake I should be grateful for the opportunity to experiment more on" – he waves his notes dismissively at Henry – "whatever you are."

The Professor looks at Stitch now, and the way the Professor speaks makes Stitch think he has forgotten there is anybody else in the room. "Stitch, on the other hand, crude as he is, is probably more complete. Ironically he provides fewer possibilities for scientific exploration. I think Henry's brain matter, defective and lacking in fusion, can explain his outbursts. I think these can be remedied by further experimentation with the machine. A proper synthesis might then be accomplished." Professor Hardacre strokes his chin. Stitch can only follow some of his meaning, but he knows he doesn't like the way Professor Hardacre is describing Henry. "Yes, I think so. It would be a fine place to start. It would help me unlock more of the secrets my uncle sought to divine; then maybe I could progress to the next stage, and..."

Professor Hardacre stops speaking, and his eyes take on a faraway look. He clutches the locket hanging around his neck.

"Professor?" says Alice, stepping towards him.

Professor Hardacre shakes his head, as if waking himself.

"Yes, yes, most definitely," he says. "I can fix you, Henry."

"Fix me?" says Henry.

"But Henry is perfectly fine," says Stitch. "Granted, he breaks things..."

Professor Hardacre is no longer listening. Instead, he's smiling and muttering to himself, slapping the pages of notes with glee. Stitch cannot understand his behaviour at all. If anything, it is even more perplexing and erratic than Henry's.

Professor Hardacre leaves the room, his excited laughter echoing along the corridor.

Alice looks strangely apologetic and guilty, even though she has not done anything to be apologetic or guilty about. It seems like she wants to say something, but thinks better of it. "I should go after him," she says quietly. Stitch nods. Alice leaves the room.

There is silence for a few moments. Stitch doesn't know what to say.

"Fix me?" Henry says. "But I am Henry Oaf, whole and complete in my..."

Henry steps back into his cage and sits on his bed, staring at the floor.

Some Bad News for Henry

$\int$titch sits beside Henry.

They are both quiet for some time. Stitch enjoys the silence between them. He realizes that because Henry is his best friend, he feels comfortable in the silence. This is something that he has never appreciated before.

"Henry?"

"Yes, Stitch."

"What are you thinking about?"

"I am thinking about the fact that I am imperfect and must be fixed."

Stitch stands up, folds his arms, and looks Henry straight in the eye.

"Henry Oaf, listen to me now."

Henry looks surprised. Stitch feels somehow

larger than he actually is, like he is a giant, capable of tearing down walls.

"You are my friend, Henry, and I hold you in the highest esteem. You are the best person I know."

"You know very few people, Stitch," says Henry, counting on his fingers.

"That may be, but of the people I know you are among the very best, and I will not have you considering yourself less than that."

Stitch gives a curt nod to signal that this is his final word on the matter. He feels strange, foolish, and yet strong: a mixture of things he hasn't felt before.

Henry looks appreciative. "Those are very fine sentiments, Stitch, and I thank you for them." He stands up. "It is good to be free," he says. "I must take advantage of the fact and go and apologize to the old Professor for my past transgressifications and bouts of mischief."

"Here's the thing, Henry," says Stitch, unable to look him in the eye.

There is silence as Henry walks around the Professor's bedroom. Stitch watches him as he touches things: ornaments and books and pieces of parchment. Henry looks into the cracked, speckled mirror over the washhand basin. He examines the window ledge, and his large body is framed by the light coming in through the window. Henry picks up a small leather-bound book and flicks through its pages, then he goes and sits on the Professor's empty bed, holding the small book in his hands. He looks around the room.

"So, the Professor is gone?" he says.

"That's right, Henry. I'm sorry. He's dead."

"Dead," says Henry. "I believe I have heard the word, although I confess I do not fully understand it. This is quite surprising because I have picked up a lot of knowledge in my own studies and assessments of the world, and I must say…"

Henry whimpers, drops the book, and covers his face with his hands. He starts sobbing.

Stitch sits with him and places a hand on his arm.

"There, there, Henry. It's all right."

Henry straightens up and wipes his eyes and

nose with the top of his hand. He tries to smile even though he has tears in his eyes.

"Well, it isn't, but it will be," he says.

He pats Stitch's hand in gratitude, then looks thoughtful.

"The thing I would like to know, Stitch, is where is the Professor gone? Where is his voice? Where is his mind? Where are his ideas and thoughts? Where are his dreams?"

"This is a question I've asked too," says Stitch.

"And have you discovered a suitable answer?"

Stitch shakes his head. "Not yet."

Henry sighs, then a sheet of paper lying on the bedside locker seems to attract his attention.

"Well, that is most interesting – my name is written on here. This appears to be one of the Professor's notes," says Henry.

Henry picks up the sheet and starts to read it, his lips moving silently, and the more he reads the more he frowns. He seems very disconcerted by whatever he has read. Not being able to read, Stitch can't tell what's written on the page, but he knows it must be of a very serious nature.

"Henry? What is it?"

Henry is still reading, and now he looks even more perturbed. Stitch's neck starts to tingle.

"Henry?"

Henry shakes his head as if to clear it. He slaps the page against the book and stands up quickly. "I think perhaps it would be best to shake myself and to go forth and deal with the endeavours of the day. All of this silly snottifying and sniffilizing will accomplish nothing."

Stitch stands up. "Right then, Henry."

Henry smiles, but he shows no willingness to leave the room. Stitch notices that he is slowly and absent-mindedly crumpling the paper in his hand.

"Stitch?"

"Yes, Henry?"

Stitch wonders if he is about to tell him what he has just read. Whatever it was must be very important.

Henry looks around the room. Stitch understands now. He forgets the sheet of paper and its mysterious words, because Henry now has the most forlorn look on his face.

"Maybe if I could take a moment alone…" says Henry.

"Of course."

Stitch leaves him in the room.

He finds it a very difficult thing to do.

The Hooded Man
and the Mysterious Box

$titch spends the rest of the day in his room. He takes out *The Great Book of Exploration* and starts to look at it. As the sky begins to fade to a sullen grey, rain spatters the window. He lights a candle, illuminating the mountains and rivers and valleys in the book. Stitch feels like he wants to dive into the pages, to explore the mountains and valleys, to be anywhere but here. He has never felt this feeling so strongly before.

When he finally looks up from his book, the sky is dark and the moon is out.

Henry will be happy, he thinks.

Then he notices the slight orange glow reflected in the raindrops on the window. He hears the *clop clop* of hooves and the familiar squeak and groan of a horse-drawn cart. It can only mean one thing.

The Hooded Man is coming.

Stitch goes to the window and looks down to see the cart making its way towards the castle. It stops just underneath his window, and the huge hulking driver clambers slowly down from his seat.

Stitch's heart almost skips a beat when he realizes he was correct. It is indeed the Hooded Man. The Hooded Man always arrives in great secrecy, and only when summoned by the Professor. The Professor employed him as an assistant of sorts, and he would often have him deliver supplies. Stitch calls him the Hooded Man because of the hood that he wears at all times. His face is almost totally covered by a cloth mask, except for a single blue eye, which Stitch cannot look at for too long because it seems to blaze with an incessant rage.

The Hooded Man is even taller and broader than Henry. He is like a walking mountain. Stitch has only ever been near him once in the laboratory.

He had smelled of soil and iron, of woods and earth, of things from the world outside.

The Hooded Man suddenly looks upwards, and for one terrifying moment Stitch finds himself staring into that blazing blue eye. He stumbles back from the window, heart pounding.

Then comes the deep BOOM BOOM of the door knocker.

Stitch steals a glance at Brown Mouse in his cage. But Brown Mouse is sleeping.

Stitch hears the door open, and the sound of voices. He knows something strange is afoot. For a while he hears nothing, then there is the steady *clomp clomp* of heavy boots making their way upstairs. The clomping comes closer and closer, until Stitch hears the boots move past his door, followed by lighter footfalls, and Professor Hardacre whispering viciously.

"*Quiet* now!"

There is a commotion near by: what sounds like furniture being moved; doors being opened and shut.

Then silence.

Stitch waits a moment, then sneaks out of his room. He walks through the castle corridors, but the castle seems empty now. Whatever is happening is not for his eyes. He wonders where everybody is.

Then he catches the glow of a lamp through a window.

Stitch makes his way down a small side corridor, knowing there is a door that will give him a good vantage point. He opens the door just a crack.

The moon illuminates the scene for him. The Hooded Man is digging a hole with Alice while Professor Hardacre looks on. There is a long wooden box beside the hole. After a while the Hooded Man and Alice stop digging, then the Hooded Man lifts the box and deposits it in the hole.

He climbs out and wipes his hands.

"You should say something," Alice says to Professor Hardacre.

Professor Hardacre snorts.

"He was your uncle," says Alice.

Stitch can see Alice looking up defiantly at Professor Hardacre. He feels a certain admiration for her.

"Very well then," says Professor Hardacre. He clears his throat. "My uncle was a good man, a true visionary. I hope I can remain faithful to his spirit of scientific enquiry, and indeed even surpass his achievements."

Alice sighs and shakes her head. Then she and the Hooded Man start shovelling soil into the hole and on top of the box.

Stitch returns to his room, and finds himself pacing back and forth, pondering what he has seen. It all seemed so very familiar and yet strange too. His eyes alight on the empty cage and he stops pacing. He stands in the centre of the room feeling lost, as if it is not his room any more, as if all its geometries and angles have changed. He looks at the marks on his wall. He reaches under the bed and takes out the slate. He kneels by the bed, looks at the chalk marks, counts them. Then, after a moment's hesitation, he wipes the slate clean with his sleeve.

When Stitch wakes up the next morning, he has only one thought on his mind. He is distracted even when feeding Brown Mouse. He looks at the empty cage and the mixture of old feelings return: the happiness, the sadness. He has a sudden vision of bright eyes, a feeling of warmth. He knows now where he's going this morning. He is going to the garden. It feels like he is being drawn by an invisible force.

When he walks through the garden, he is so wrapped up in thinking about his final destination that he jumps when someone calls his name.

"Stitch."

He turns to find Alice fixing him with that strangely powerful look she has: the one that is unflinching, as if she can read his thoughts. For a moment Stitch feels a sense of panic, but he quells it by reminding himself that nobody can read minds.

"Your nose," says Alice.

Stitch tilts his head and touches his nose.

"What about it?" he asks, feeling utterly confused.

"It makes a whistling sound when you're nervous."

Stitch tries to chuckle. "Why, that is an interesting observation, Alice. One that I would never have made myself. When might I be nervous?"

"When you're sneaking a peek through doorways late at night."

Alice just looks at him. Stitch feels that sense of panic rising again. His face feels hot.

"It's all right," says Alice. "No one else noticed."

"Why didn't you say anything?"

Alice shrugs. "I know what it's like to sneak around and try not to be seen."

Stitch is intrigued. "Why would you try not to be seen?"

Alice looks slightly uncomfortable for a moment.

"Have you ever been outside, Stitch?"

"Of course, quite a bit. Especially around the garden."

"No, I mean have you ever been in the outside world?"

"You mean further than the garden?"

"Yes."

Stitch shakes his head.

"Well then, that's probably a good thing."

"How could that be a good thing, Alice?"

"It's hard to explain, but I suppose the world is not always the nicest place."

Stitch nods. "Of course. I understand. Because of weather."

Alice looks confused. "What?"

"Weather. It can be quite unpredictable. It might be sunny at first, then it might snow, and you might get caught in a blizzard. I've read about such things in *The Great Book of Exploration* – or rather, Henry has read it to me. I'd like to be an explorer someday, to go out into the world, despite the weather. In fact, I think the weather might make exploring more interesting and exciting." Stitch looks at the window, and now he imagines himself in an isolated tundra, wrapped in furs, surrounded by a vast whiteness. He looks to the imaginary horizon.

"I was talking about people," says Alice.

Stitch blinks and comes out of his reverie. "What's that?"

"People. They tend to make the world … not the nicest place. Especially when you're like me. Especially when you have nothing."

Stitch frowns. "Don't you like people, Alice?"

Alice looks uneasy. "It's not that it's *all* people, but if you've had the life I've had… If you haven't been in the outside world, I suppose it might be hard to understand."

Stitch grins. "I like people. I don't know many, but I like them. I like you especially, Alice. You are pleasant and friendly, and I feel I can trust you."

For a moment Alice looks at him in an odd way, almost as if she can't believe that Stitch is standing right there before her. Eventually she smiles.

"Thank you, Stitch. That's very nice of you to say. I like you too. You're very kind; that counts for a lot. I suppose I haven't met many kind people. And you're part of the world, so in a sense you make the world better."

"Then I have helped you in some way, Alice."

Alice's smile broadens. "Yes, I suppose you have."

"Why did you bury the wooden box, Alice?"

Alice looks momentarily surprised by his sudden change of tack.

"It was a coffin, Stitch. The Professor's remains were in it. That's what happens when people pass away: we have a ceremonial burial and say words of consolation."

Stitch feels strange. It's as if the world wobbles for a moment and is then still. Things are beginning to make sense to him now. Alice doesn't seem to notice the brief change in his thoughts. Stitch is reassured.

"I'm sorry about what the Professor did yesterday. He's a bully, Stitch," says Alice. "He likes to break people down and bend them to his will."

"He shouldn't have spoken to Henry like that."

"It's easier for him to belittle someone like Henry," says Alice.

"Why?"

"Because Henry is different."

"Everyone is different, Alice. I've told you that. It's what the Professor would have called *self-evident*."

Alice looks intrigued. "Is that what you think, Stitch? That everyone is just different and that's it? What about the way the world treats those they think are more different than most?"

This idea puzzles Stitch. He scratches his head.

"But everyone is just … different."

Alice raises an eyebrow. "If that's all you think then you are either very foolish or very wise."

Stitch doesn't know what to say to this.

"Why was Henry kept in a cage?" It is Alice's turn to change the subject.

"Henry is excitabub ... I mean, excitable." Stitch looks at the ground. "And Henry breaks things," he adds darkly.

"What do you mean?"

Stitch doesn't want to tell her because telling her would make him think about it, but he has a feeling in his heart now – a feeling that he wants to lift a weight from himself. It is not something he has ever felt before, but Alice is nice, and even though he has known her only a very short time, he knows that she is his friend.

Besides, he has already decided on his destination, the place he is drawn to. The place he has avoided for quite some time. Everything Alice has told him about the burial has reminded him of the place, and something he did some time ago. Something secret. Perhaps Alice can accompany him.

He takes a deep breath. He makes his decision.

"Follow me," he says.

He takes her through the garden, past the vivid red flowers and bushes brimming with berries and the tall drooping green plants that give shade on sunny days.

He takes her to the small mound at the back of the grounds. The small green mound on which pebbles are arranged in the shape of a circle. The small green mound that seemed so inexplicable so long ago, but now makes perfect sense.

He looks at Alice.

"This is the story of Henry and White Rabbit," he says.

The Story of Henry and White Rabbit

The favourite part of Stitch's day was always the time he spent with White Rabbit. From the first moment Stitch saw White Rabbit's pink eyes and his twitchy little nose he knew they would be firm friends. The Professor said White Rabbit was for his experiments, but Stitch told the Professor that he believed White Rabbit's time would be better spent with Stitch. To that end he begged the Professor to let him keep him. The Professor finally relented. He tried to be stern, but as soon as he handed White Rabbit over to Stitch, his face broke into his familiar crinkly smile.

Stitch kept White Rabbit in a cage in his room. He would feed White Rabbit a lettuce leaf and some carrot.

He would watch him drink from a saucer of water, and the sight would always brighten his morning. After White Rabbit had been fed, Stitch would take him out of his cage and sit with him for a while, stroking and talking to him, and telling him about his hopes for the day.

"I want to go and see the flowers today, and then maybe I will have a chat with Henry, and I might help the Professor with his experiments."

White Rabbit was a great listener. His fur was warm, his movements lively and quick. Once Stitch let him loose among the flowers and he laughed as White Rabbit bounced among the greenery, and Stitch got down on his hands and knees and copied his movements. White Rabbit made him happy, and somehow, even though he couldn't speak, Stitch knew that White Rabbit was happy to be in his company too.

One day he was walking through the castle, cradling White Rabbit in his arms. He could hear Henry bounding and crashing about, which was something he did from time to time. He could hear the Professor shouting, "Henry! Stop that now!" but the noise continued, and through it all he could hear Henry doing his big silly guffaw – the laugh he did when he became "excitabubble".

Stitch went outside to the great stone step. The air was warm, the sun was shining. He sat with White Rabbit in his lap, stroking him, feeling the warmth of his fur, the nibbledy nobblediness of his bones, the twitch twitch *of him.*

"'Allo, Stitch! What, may I ask, are you doing currently in this moment in time?"

Henry's voice came from above. Stitch looked up to see him idly swinging back and forth, one-handed, from a turret.

"White Rabbit and I were just sitting here, Henry."

Henry let go of the turret, dropped a few feet, grabbed a cornice, see-sawed back and forth, and then launched himself through the air.

He landed a few feet in front of Stitch, his momentum propelling him forward with such speed that he had to do a little pointy-toed jog to bring himself to a stop. He giggled as he did this, and Stitch smiled.

"Oh, Stitch," he gasped, leaning with his hands on his thighs as he tried to catch his breath. "You have to try ... you have to... Ah hur hur..." He wheezed as he pointed at the roof.

He was convulsed again with another round of giggles and his head waggled back and forth and he beat his chest in his happy delirium. Stitch waited for him to calm down a little.

Henry wiped his eyes. "Oh," was all he could say for a while. "Oh."

He grinned at Stitch. "So, what have you been doing, Stitch?"

"Just sitting here with White Rabbit."

Henry frowned. "I mean no offence to White Rabbit, but surely he is not the greatest of company, what with him being incapable of the rudiments of speechifying and verbalirization."

"If you mean him not being able to talk is a shortcoming, then the truth is I have found that not to be the case."

Henry sat beside Stitch, still frowning as he looked at White Rabbit.

"Then tell me, Stitch, what special quality is it that White Rabbit brings to any interaction between him and your good self?"

Stitch stroked White Rabbit. "He is soft and warm, and I find the way he moves and looks about most pleasing and amusing. He is very good company, Henry."

Henry seemed to consider this, then he put out his hands.

"May I?"

Stitch felt strangely reluctant for a moment, but then he looked at Henry with his mop of hair and his soft friendly eyes, and he nodded.

"Of course."

He gently handed White Rabbit to Henry. Henry cupped White Rabbit in his huge hands and laid him on his lap. Henry looked confused. Stitch reached out a hand and started to stroke White Rabbit.

"Like this," he said.

Henry watched closely, then he too started to stroke White Rabbit. Stitch noticed that Henry's breathing was getting slower as he stroked White Rabbit. He almost seemed to be in a trance. He stroked White Rabbit slowly and gently. His mouth open in awe.

He looked at Stitch and smiled. "You were right, Stitch. He is very good company indeed."

Stitch smiled back. Henry giggled. His shoulders shook as he giggled. The giggle turned into one of his big deep gurgling laughs. Stitch felt a flicker of anxiety.

"Henry—"

Henry grabbed White Rabbit between his two hands and raised him up in the air and gaped at him.

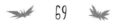 69

"Look at him, Stitch. Isn't he wonderful? Look at how his little nose twitches. He is most amusing and congenial in manner. Ah hur hur hur."

Stitch tried to lay a hand on Henry's arm to calm him, but Henry stood up quickly.

"He is my friend now, and as my friend I think it behoves me to show him the sights and sounds of my abode so that he may get to know me better and understand me and that our bond will be strengthened by such sharing."

Stitch jumped up. "Henry, please…"

But Henry was already running away into the castle, whooping and laughing.

Stitch ran after him, but Henry was fast and agile, leaping over furniture, swinging from giant chandeliers — until he disappeared deep into the bowels of the castle.

Stitch spent some time trying to find him, all the while his heart fluttering in a panic. Eventually he found him in a storeroom. Henry was sitting on a stool with his back turned to the door.

"Henry?"

Henry didn't turn around at first. "Stitch," was all he said, but his voice was low and flat, and all the giddiness seemed to have drained from it.

Stitch went towards him feeling a great sense of unease.

Henry's eyes were fixed on White Rabbit in his lap as he stroked him.

"I was petting him," said Henry. "But he must have been tired because he appears to have gone to sleep."

Henry gave a nervous smile, but Stitch could see tears brimming in his eyes.

White Rabbit's eyes were wide open, but they were glazed now, and his whole body was limp.

"I can't wake him up, Stitch," sobbed Henry.

"Henry broke White Rabbit," says Stitch.

They are both quiet for a moment as they look at the mound.

"He didn't mean to, but he broke him all the same," says Stitch. "I tried to wake him up too, but White Rabbit was cold…"

A sudden wave of sadness overcomes Stitch. He covers his face with his arm. He feels Alice's hand squeeze his shoulder.

"The Professor said that Henry would have to be locked up until he had learned his lesson. Henry was always breaking things because he didn't know his own strength, he said. He said being kept locked up for a while would teach him to stop breaking things."

Stitch kneels before the mound. He touches it with his hand.

"Why did you bury him, Stitch?"

Stitch shrugs. "It felt like the right thing to do. And now, after all I saw last night, it all makes sense."

Alice kneels beside him.

"Henry didn't mean to do it. He just doesn't know his own strength," he says again, the line so familiar now. He has said it many times.

Stitch turns to Alice. "White Rabbit is gone, just like the Professor."

Alice nods.

"I'm sorry to ask again. I know I ask many questions. But where did they go?" Stitch says, as he looks up into the sky.

Stitch is surprised when Alice takes his hand. She places it over his heart.

"They went here," she says. She gently touches the side of his head. "And here."

Stitch thinks about this. He doesn't fully understand, but Alice's smile is comfort enough for him.

"You are very kind, Alice. And hard too, like a flinty rock. You seem like two people."

Alice seems taken aback. She turns away for a moment and twists a blade of grass around her finger thoughtfully.

"The world is hard, Stitch, and when you're like us you have to be hard back. My parents left me when I was a baby. I was scrabbling around the streets for food when the Professor took me in."

"So he is a good man, despite all."

"Maybe, deep down."

"And bad. He is bad also."

"Only because the world was hard to him too. I feel sorry for him in a way."

"Why?"

"Because he had no one either. His wife and child died a few years ago. It was only after that that he became obsessed with his uncle's experiments. He would lock himself in his study and read those letters over and over, and write back pages and pages."

Stitch thinks about this; how terrible it must be to lose two people. He has only lost White Rabbit and the Professor, and even that was nearly unendurable.

"You lost your parents. You might be two people because of it, but both people are good people, Alice."

Alice gives a grudging smile. "Thank you, Stitch."

Stitch stands up. Alice follows suit.

"Words of consolation," he says.

Alice nods. She takes his hand. Stitch clears his throat.

"Goodbye, White Rabbit. You were a good friend and I miss you. Goodbye also, Professor. You were a good Professor, and I miss you too."

Stitch looks out over the garden. A soft breeze stirs the flowers. They both stand like that for a few moments, and Stitch feels sad but happy too, knowing that he has said his words.

The Machine

Alice tells Stitch that Professor Hardacre wants to see them in the laboratory. They find Professor Hardacre with his shirt sleeves rolled up and wearing the old Professor's leather apron. For some reason, when Stitch sees him wearing the apron, he feels a slight twinge of resentment.

"Good morning, Stitch. I was hoping you could help me."

Professor Hardacre is wiping his oily hands with a cloth. He appears to have been tinkering with the machine. The machine is a large hulking metal box fitted with levers and dials. It is attached by lengths of wire to the table in the centre of the laboratory. There are winches attached to the corners of the table so that it can be raised or lowered by pulling a lever that protrudes from the floor.

"I shall do my very best, Professor," says Stitch.

The Professor smiles at him again, but it is one of those smiles that somehow makes Stitch feel small.

"I take it you know what the machine does?"

Stitch frowns as he looks at the machine. For a moment his mind is filled with the image of spidery lightning, and he can see it arcing above him along the chains and wheels of the winches, and he can feel it tingling, and his eyes open wide, and the world floods in...

"It wakes people up," says Stitch.

The Professor chuckles. "Wakes people up. Very good, how droll."

"Stitch is only learning about things that are new to him."

Professor Hardacre looks at Alice. His eyebrows scrunch together. His eyes darken.

"Alice, when I need you to speak—"

"Life and death are things he's only recently discovered," says Alice.

The Professor looks at Stitch, then nods slowly. "Of course, then we must teach him. Tell me, Stitch, you talk about waking. What did you mean by that?"

Stitch shrugs. "Why waking of course. Like I do every day."

"Have you heard of the concept of birth?" Alice talks gently to Stitch. "It wasn't that you woke, Stitch. You came to life."

Stitch feels that odd unsteady feeling again. Both Alice and the Professor are looking at him strangely. He is trying his very best to understand what is going on.

Life. Death. Birth. Waking. He finds it a lot to take in.

He has a sudden thought.

"Where was I before?"

"Before what?" asks Professor Hardacre.

"Before waking."

"That's a very interesting question, Stitch. And in your case one with a rather complicated answer."

He seems amused again. Stitch is beginning to feel uncomfortable every time Professor Hardacre looks amused. It feels as if he is not being let in on a joke and that perhaps the joke is about him.

"It would take some considerable time to explain. We would have to cover many varying disciplines, between science, philosophy, religion." He shakes his head. "So much to cover, Stitch. I doubt your little brain could take it all in one huge indigestible chunk. I think perhaps we shall proceed slowly with your education."

Stitch notices that Alice is glowering at Professor Hardacre, but Hardacre is too busy looking pleased as he surveys the laboratory.

"We will accomplish great deeds here, Stitch. Great deeds."

The next few days are a whirlwind of moments spent mainly in the laboratory. Professor Hardacre measures and weighs both Stitch and Henry. He spends a lot of time going through his uncle's notes. He has Stitch, Henry and Alice carry lots of extra equipment into the laboratory. As the days pass, Stitch notes how frantic Professor Hardacre seems – almost feverish with excitement.

On the third day of "research", he walks into the laboratory to find Professor Hardacre holding a flaming Bunsen burner to the palm of Henry's hand. Henry doesn't seem too bothered. "'Allo, Stitch," he says cheerily. Stitch notices that Alice is glowering as she sorts through some test tubes.

"According to my uncle's notes, you're both remarkably resilient, Stitch. Extremes of heat and cold don't affect you in the way they might affect us."

Henry giggles. "That tickles, Mr Professor's Nephew."

Hardacre turns to Stitch with the Bunsen burner. The flame is an icy blue.

"Would you like a demonstration?"

"No, he wouldn't," says Alice.

Stitch sees the stern look Professor Hardacre gives Alice, but he also notes the way Alice returns his look without flinching.

Professor Hardacre switches the burner off. He smiles at Stitch. "Alice has a certain way about her. It's not an attitude I like to encourage." He smirks at her. "She would do well to remember how much she owes me."

"I stuck my hand in a bucket of ice for two hours, Stitch," says Henry. "It was most refreshing."

The Hooded Man clomps into the laboratory. He has been coming more often lately. He is carrying something covered by a shroud. As the Hooded Man walks past Stitch, it feels as if the air itself parts for him – such is his huge height. He puts the object on a table, almost dropping it at the last minute.

"Be careful with that!" shouts Professor Hardacre.

The Hooded Man straightens up and looks at him with that single blue eye.

"Now get out," says Professor Hardacre.

For a second that seems like it's lasting for ever, the Hooded Man just looks at Professor Hardacre. He eventually turns and leaves the laboratory.

Professor Hardacre looks disdainful "Clearly an imbecile," he mutters, "albeit a useful one."

He uncovers the object on the table. Stitch recognizes it as something the Professor was very proud of. It is a large brass device with a dial inset into the side that looks like a clock face with many numbers and hands. A tangled messy spiral of wires protrudes upwards from the base. This is what the Professor called his "lightning detector". His nephew seems just as taken with it.

"Can you feel that?" says Professor Hardacre, holding up his index finger.

Stitch hesitantly raises his own index finger in response, but he doesn't feel anything.

"A storm is coming, Stitch. And with my uncle's most marvellous contraption I can pinpoint the optimum moment. The perfect time!"

"Perfect time for what?" Stitch asks.

Professor Hardacre gestures at the table in the centre of the room. "Why, for the great experiment! Henry's shining hour."

Henry nods. He clenches and unclenches his fingers and tries his best to smile, but Stitch can always tell when Henry is uncomfortable.

Stitch looks at the table upon which he emerged into the world. He sees the steel cables that extend from the corners like the tentacles of an octopus, a picture of which he once saw in *The Great Book of Exploration*. The cables are now attached to the metal pole that rises upwards to the high ceiling. The pole is extended by the turning of a crank and chain mechanism, until its very tip lifts through the metal flap at the centre of the skylights that look down upon the laboratory.

The sky through the windows today is murky and grey. The clouds almost seem to be bubbling. Stitch reckons that rain cannot be far away.

Professor Hardacre looks upwards, his hands on his hips. "My uncle's detector seems to be in working order. All the indicators are that we shall have lightning tomorrow night. I can already feel a storm brewing. Soon the heavens will reach their boiling point, and then…"

He slaps his hands together with a great crack that makes Stitch jump.

Professor Hardacre smiles at Henry. "You should get some rest, Henry. You have a big day ahead of you. Alice, please escort Henry out."

Henry looks agitated. Alice takes him by the arm and Stitch notices the anxious glance he gives the table just before Alice leads him out of the laboratory. Stitch is worried about him.

Professor Hardacre is scribbling in a notebook, smiling to himself. Stitch approaches him.

"Excuse me, Professor," he says.

"Yes, Stitch," he says, without looking up.

Stitch spies the open locket on the desk in front of Professor Hardacre. From where he's standing, he can just about make out what looks like a picture in it. A picture of a woman and a girl.

"I was wondering, Professor, what exactly does the experiment involve, and is it absolutely necessary for Henry to take part in it?"

Professor Hardacre, still writing, lets out a snort. "Take part? Henry *is* the experiment. I will be attempting to fuse the disparate and disconnected parts of his brain, so that he may function better as a person and be less erratic in his behaviour."

"I think Henry functions quite well as a person as he is," says Stitch.

The Professor looks up with an expression of mild amusement, which quickly changes to panic when he realizes that Stitch has seen the locket. He grabs the locket, snaps it shut, and deposits it in his waistcoat pocket.

"It's just that Henry seems reluctant to be involved."

"I hadn't noticed," says Professor Hardacre drily, returning to his jottings.

"Why are you here, Professor Hardacre?"

The Professor looks as surprised by the question as Stitch feels by his asking of it.

"I'm an explorer, Stitch."

Stitch tilts his head. "I have a book about explorers. Henry gave it to me. It has pictures of explorers. You don't look like an explorer."

Professor Hardacre chuckles. "I mean an explorer of scientific possibilities. Henry will be my first step upon a grand path. Once I discover how to correct him, I will have the necessary raw information to explore even more." He makes a fist. "I want to reach into the heart of things and divine the secrets that lie at the heart of all creation."

"Why?"

"So that I can control them."

"Control *what*, exactly?"

Professor Hardacre looks into the middle distance and answers quietly. "Life. Death."

Stitch ponders this for a moment as the Professor looks lost in his own imaginings. Try as he might, he still comes back to the same question.

"But why?"

"Does there have to be a why?"

"Well … yes. I think there's a *why* for everything. Why is Henry my friend? Because we like each other. Why is Alice my friend? Because she is wise and kind. Why are you Alice's friend? Because maybe you thought she needed one when she was alone in the world. Why is Alice your friend? Because she feels sorry for you."

Professor Hardacre looks stunned for a moment, then angry.

"Get out," he snaps.

"But Professor Hardacre, there is still the matter of why. And also, Henry; I think it might be worth considering his feelings and—"

"I said get out!"

Stitch doesn't understand what made the Professor so angry, nor does he understand why he felt the need to suddenly hide the locket, but Stitch feels that all these odd things that Professor Hardacre does are somehow connected. He takes one last look at him as he leaves the laboratory, scribbling away frantically, muttering to himself, and just for a moment it looks like Professor Hardacre is fighting back tears.

That night, in his bedroom, Stitch watches lightning illuminate the far horizon. He can't hear the rumble of thunder yet, but he knows it is there. He goes to bed, and dreams deep. He dreams of the First Day, of looking up at the ceiling in the laboratory, of lightning and a feeling of newness and freshness, of seeing wood and stone for the first time and a voice saying, "Welcome."

Then he dreams of something else. Something darker. And in the dark he hears a voice simply say, "No."

The voice belongs to Henry.

The Great Experiment

Thunder rumbles outside. It has been building in intensity all day, and Stitch can feel it pulsing through the very stones of the castle. It has brought with it an unnatural darkness even before sunset. The air feels sticky and heavy in the laboratory as Stitch helps Professor Hardacre with his equipment. Alice has gone to fetch Henry. The Hooded Man is watching from a gantry just above the machine. Stitch wonders why he is here, especially considering he seems to have done all that was asked of him. Professor Hardacre seems to have forgotten him.

Alice arrives. She is leading Henry by the hand.

Lightning flashes, illuminating everything in a harsh white glow for just a moment. Stitch sees Henry flinch. Alice whispers words of comfort to him.

Stitch notices the dial of the lightning detector bouncing back and forth with greater speed with each passing moment.

"Yes! Yes!" Professor Hardacre shouts with glee as the indicator almost becomes a blur. He scribbles one final note, then slaps his notebook down on his desk. He flicks some switches, throws two small levers.

The laboratory hums into life, great rotors turn and whirr, the walls and floor hum. Stitch can feel his stomach lurching. His hair feels like it is standing on end. He watches Henry gaping at the machinery. Above, on the gantry, the Hooded Man shuffles back and forth for a second, as if contemplating leaving.

Professor Hardacre gestures towards the table at the centre of the room, like a magician ushering his assistant towards a magical device. "Henry, if you would be so kind."

Henry swallows, steps forward, then stops. He shakes his head vigorously.

"No thank you, Mr Professor's Nephew. I've had some time to think about this, and I believe my most preferred option would be not to participate in this no doubt very important scientificacious experiment thank you very much indeed – and goodbye."

Henry turns to go, but he is stopped in his tracks by Professor Hardacre bellowing, "Henry!"

Henry looks at him. Professor Hardacre holds up some notes. "Do you know what this is, Henry?"

Henry seems to gain some measure of bravery from what sounds like a very simple question with a very simple answer. He chuckles.

"I think I have the sense in me to recognize pieces of paper when I observalize suchlike at close proximity."

Professor Hardacre's smile makes Stitch feel uneasy. He feels the sudden panicked urge to tell Henry to stop talking.

"No, Henry. This is not just pieces of paper. This is you." Professor Hardacre starts to read a word from each page, and as he reads he scrunches each sheet up and throws it away. "Incomplete. Deficient. Irregular. Flawed. Wrong."

Henry frowns. His lips twitch, but he can't seem to utter words. Stitch notes that Alice looks angry. She goes to speak, but Professor Hardacre holds his hand up and snarls at her. "Oh no, not this time, Alice."

Professor Hardacre steps towards Henry. He reads from the final sheet of paper.

"Defective."

He crumples the paper up and throws it over his shoulder. Henry watches the flight of the scrap of paper with a mournful look on his face. Stitch feels a twisting in his gut.

"Look at you, a mishmash of things, a pile of odds and ends, a calamitous collection of parts that don't fit together."

Henry has tears in his eyes.

"Do you want to be defective, Henry?"

Henry shakes his head.

"Wouldn't you prefer not to break things? Important things? Things like White Rabbit?"

Henry looks shocked, and Stitch feels just as shocked by the mention of White Rabbit. He looks at Alice, and for once she doesn't seem to be able to look him in the eye.

"Don't you want to be better?" asks Professor Hardacre, touching Henry's arm.

Henry nods, avoiding Hardacre's gaze.

"Well then, it's settled."

He steps aside for Henry. Another lightning flash illuminates the laboratory. Alice exchanges a glance with Stitch. It is full of guilt. He knows this because she looks away again so quickly. Stitch is still reeling slightly from the fact that she told Professor Hardacre about White Rabbit. He feels as if too much is happening at once, and the world seems to be filled with a buzzing sound.

Henry moves towards the centre of the room like a condemned man.

Professor Hardacre gestures at Stitch. "It's time, Stitch."

For some reason Stitch can't seem to move his legs. The buzzing in his head is getting louder. He watches Henry lie down on the table. Professor Hardacre glares at Stitch.

"Stitch, come now. Do as I showed you."

Stitch goes to the table. He straps Henry's wrists and ankles, just as Professor Hardacre showed him. He places the metal skullcap on Henry's head, just as Professor Hardacre demonstrated. He does all of this mechanically, while trying to ignore the fact that Henry's chest is going up and down rapidly while Henry's eyes move quickly from side to side.

"Mr Professor's Nephew, sir, if I may ask you a most pertinent question?" says Henry.

Professor Hardacre is checking some dials. "You may."

"Will I be different?" asks Henry.

"You will be better, Henry."

Henry looks at Stitch now, his eyes wide. He speaks in a low voice filled with fear, and it makes Stitch feel sick.

"Better is different, Stitch. I don't want to be different. I want to be me."

Stitch steps away from the table. His palms are sweating. Lightning flashes again. Stitch notices the indicator of the lightning detector is now a blur. He looks at Alice but Alice is avoiding his gaze.

"Stitch! To your post," Professor Hardacre shouts.

Stitch takes his position by the lever protruding from the floor. Professor Hardacre stands before the machine; he frantically turns a large metal wheel, and now the air is shrieking with the sound of the laboratory's great mechanisms turning, the low dull moan of arcane machinery, and above it all the rumbling thunder, and the lightning now flashing with greater frequency. Stitch's forehead feels damp. He wipes it. He spies the Hooded Man leaning forward, his gloved hands tightening on the handrail.

"It's time!" Professor Hardacre bellows to the others. He runs towards a panel and throws a switch. Alice positions herself by another switch. There is a screeching sound from the machine.

"Now!" he shrieks.

Alice flicks the switch. Stitch pulls the lever towards him.

The table rises towards the ceiling. The windows open. Rain falls through, lightning crackles across the night sky. Stitch can no longer see Henry's face. He cannot take his eyes off the table as it rises. The buzzing in his head is impossibly loud now, but beneath it he can hear the echo of Henry's voice in his head.

"Will I be different?"

The windows in the ceiling part. The table continues its ascent towards the boiling black sky veined with lightning.

There is crack upon crack of thunder, as if the very walls of the castle are going to split open. Then lightning flashes, blazing with an insistent brightness Stitch has never witnessed before.

All it will take is one lightning bolt to hit the table. In his mind's eye Stitch can see it arcing towards Henry.

"I don't want to be different."

Stitch pushes the lever back. The table starts to descend, just as lightning races through the opening, filling up the space where the table had been moments before, twisting outwards looking for purchase and finding only the stone walls, spitting and arcing against it, throwing down a torrent of sparks and brick dust that showers down on Professor Hardacre.

"NO!" the Professor screams, his snarling face turned in Stitch's direction as he flaps at the sparks that fall upon him.

The table crashes back to earth. Stitch runs towards it. He starts to undo Henry's bonds.

Stitch manages to free one of Henry's enormous hands before Professor Hardacre barges into him, sending him sprawling across the floor. Then the Professor looms over Stitch.

"How dare you! Do you know what you've done?"

Stitch stands up. "I think so. I think I may very well have stopped something that Henry didn't want to be part of."

There is a rumble of thunder, but it seems distant now. Professor Hardacre looks upwards, an expression of anguish on his face.

"The moment is gone!" he cries.

Henry is freed from the table thanks to Alice, who helps him while the Professor's back is turned. He moves contritely towards the Professor.

"I must apologize, Mr Professor's Nephew, but I felt that—"

Professor Hardacre slaps Henry across the face.

For a moment Hardacre looks as surprised as Henry, then he slaps him again. Henry cowers against the table as Hardacre rains down blow after blow.

One moment Stitch is watching all of this in disbelief. The next he is standing between Professor Hardacre and Henry without even knowing how he got there.

"You leave Henry alone!" he shouts.

Stitch has never shouted like this before, and his whole body feels suffused with a wild energy as if he might explode. Professor Hardacre looks slightly stunned, but then he draws his hand back, readying to slap Stitch.

Stitch raises himself up to his full height.

Professor Hardacre hesitates, then lowers his hand. He stumbles backwards as if in shock. Henry takes advantage of this distraction and bolts from the room. Stitch calls after him, but is met with silence.

Professor Hardacre is wandering around as if in a daze.

"This was to be my first step on the path to a scientific achievement that would change everything." He wrings his hands in a very agitated manner. "My uncle has made mistakes, but I knew if I could fuse this oaf's randomly selected constituent parts together that I could unlock so much more."

"Life and death," Stitch whispers.

From the corner, the Hooded Man makes an odd sound, like a low hoarse moan.

Professor Hardacre is now holding the locket and beating a steady rhythm against his chest with his fist. Stitch watches him. He feels as if there is something he does not understand; something that is just out of reach. He shakes his head and decides right now he has something more pressing to do than understand the Professor.

He must check on his friend.

Henry Does Something Inexplicabubble

Stitch panics because for some time, Henry is nowhere to be found. He checks the hallway, the drawing room, even the storeroom. Then he realizes there is one room he hasn't checked.

He finds Henry back in his cage, holding the small book he'd been looking at in the Professor's bedroom.

Stitch doesn't say a word. He just sits beside Henry and waits a while. The air seems clear and light now that the storm has passed.

When Henry speaks, he is still looking at the book.

"Thank you for what you did, Stitch."

Stitch just nods. He is wary about interrupting Henry because Henry's brow is wrinkled as he looks at the book, and whenever Henry's brow wrinkles like this Stitch knows he has something important to say, and it's always best to let him say it.

Henry peruses the words and pictures in the book. It seems to Stitch that the book gives him some comfort after his experience in the laboratory. Stitch is glad of it.

"The Professor showed me this book, Stitch. He taught me how to read." Henry frowns. "Or at least he *reminded* me how to."

Stitch thinks this is a peculiar thing to say. How could Henry have been *reminded* how to read? Indeed, how and when could he have forgotten in the first place?

Henry points at a very elaborate illustration on one page.

"This is a window, Stitch. It is a window in a building called a church. A church that isn't very far from here."

Stitch looks at the picture. It has many intricate designs. Stitch has never seen anything so beautiful before.

"The window is made from special glass," says Henry. "Glass of multifarious colours, and it depictorizes the beginning of everything."

"The beginning of everything," Stitch gasps. He tries to imagine it. Everything. The whole world he knows. The castle on the mountain, the trees and flowers that surround it. The villagers, the buildings they live in, and the world beyond. This place and more. His mind can barely contain it all, but when he concentrates on the picture he can see these things, all of them intertwined. They are so vibrant, he feels as if the page might burst into life.

"Everything that ever was," says Henry, and even though he is describing something monumental and beautiful, his tone seems rather sad. "Things are born, and then they grow, and then, after a time, all things die and become dead things. But I don't think Mr Professor's Nephew sees it that way. He is like his uncle, I think. He seeks a way to bring things back to life."

Henry reaches under his pillow and takes out the crumpled sheet of paper, which Stitch recognizes as the piece of paper that Henry read in the Professor's bedroom. The same piece of paper that seemed to disturb him greatly. The piece of paper with Henry's name on it.

Stitch's scalp starts to tingle. His mouth feels dry.

"This is part of the Professor's notes, Stitch. It mentions us both by name. It tells of our making and how we came to be. And what we truly are."

Stitch is afraid to ask the question, but he feels he must or he might burst.

"What are we, Henry?" he asks.

Henry shrugs, but his tone is dark.

"We are made from dead things, Stitch."

Stitch feels like the air has suddenly whooshed out of him. He is light-headed again. He gazes up at the dark window. All of it dark. Inky black; empty. He suddenly feels as if he is spinning in that darkness.

Henry raises his own hands and looks at them.

"Dead things brought to life by the power of lightning. Cobbled together I am, from bits and pieces, odds and ends, a mishmash of parts of other people. That's what the Professor's notes tell me."

He taps the side of his head. "And nothing is more hodgepodged than my own brain, which I also ascertain to be a mixture of different sources.

"Sometimes I feel like I know more than I should. At other times I know little. I know how to wield a hammer and anvil. I know certain computations of numbers that I find pleasing, and at other times their meaning eludes me. And sometimes songs and words of poetry come to me, and are then lost, and I grasp for them again, like a branch floating away from me downstream, snatched by wind and water."

Henry taps the book with his index finger.

"Hodgepodge Henry Oaf. A mixture of bits and pieces of different people, which goes some way to explaining my more inexplicabubble bouts of mischief and liveliness. And now, after all this time, a part of my brain has fully ascertainized what we are and how we came to be."

Stitch thinks about what Henry has said. He looks at his own hands, one bigger than the other. He runs a finger along one of the marks on his face.

"We are made from dead things."

Stitch thinks about the picture of the window. He can see the profusion of plants and animals and flowers and people. The vision disappears, and now all he can see in his mind's eye is lightning. The very same lightning that on the First Day brought him into this world.

Stitch feels very strange. At first he was frightened by Henry's revelation, as if something ominous was approaching. But everything seems a little sharper to him now, as if the world has taken on a new brightness. The pressure he felt as he entered Henry's room seems to have lifted. And despite all the events of tonight and the disclosure of this dark secret, Stitch can't help but smile.

"Thank you, Henry."

"For what?"

"For telling me the truth. For being my friend."

Henry smiles. "I'll always be your friend, Stitch. Of that you can be certain. Henry Oaf and Stitch. Friends for ever."

Henry puts the book and paper under his pillow, then stands up with an air of great purpose.

"Now, if you'll excuse me, Stitch, I have some important business to attend to."

Stitch smiles. "You need to talk to the moon."

Henry salutes him, then goes to the window and looks up into the night sky.

Stitch leaves him there, but before he goes he takes one last look at Henry. He feels a sense of contentment looking upon him, knowing that Henry is his friend, and that they will always be together.

Stitch wakes the next morning to a bright day. His window might be grubby, but the sky beyond is a startling blue. He makes his mark upon the wall, then feeds Brown Mouse. His eyes wander to the empty cage without hesitation. He sighs.

After talking to Brown Mouse for a bit, he makes his way downstairs. That's when he hears someone shouting. He follows the sound to the study. There he finds a dishevelled Professor Hardacre sitting at the table while Alice watches him from the door. The lightning detector is on the table beside him, mangled almost beyond recognition.

Professor Hardacre looks up. He has deep bags under his eyes. He smiles bitterly.

"Ah, Stitch. Come to admire your friend's handiwork?"

He gestures at the remains on the table.

"Henry did this?"

"Who else? Not content with merely running away, he decided to make it almost impossible for me to continue my work."

"Running away? Is this true, Alice? Has Henry run away?"

"Yes," she replies. "We can't find him anywhere."

"But..." Stitch is stunned by this news. For a moment his mind is all a flurry, then he suddenly realizes something. He turns to Professor Hardacre.

"You did this, Professor. It's because of you that he ran away. You should never have hit him. Henry is good and kind and doesn't deserve that kind of treatment."

"Would someone who is good and kind do *this*?" says the Professor, gesturing at the remains of the device on the table. The Professor leans back in his chair, his face twisted in fury. He grips the locket around his neck.

"I'll find your friend, and when I do I'll make him regret ever running away. Then we will continue my experiments, and you will help me."

Professor Hardacre starts to tinker with the lightning detector. Stitch shakes his head.

"No," he says.

Professor Hardacre looks surprised, then he snorts at him. "No? What do you mean, no?"

"I mean no as in, no I won't help you, Professor. I don't know exactly what it is you are doing, but it feels wrong. I am very sorry."

Professor Hardacre looks shocked by Stitch's words, although Stitch does notice that Alice is nodding slightly, and she has a trace of a smile on her face.

Stitch leaves the room. He feels odd, and Professor Hardacre comes to the door and shouts after him, but his shouting seems echoed and far away.

Stitch is dazed. The events of last night and this morning seem so huge. And now Henry is gone? *Surely not*, he thinks. *Surely he is just hiding again.*

He wanders back to his room. He looks out of the window at the sky, the green trees, the hazy blue of the distant mountains.

He picks up *The Great Book of Exploration*. He flicks through some of its pages, and that's when he realizes what he must do.

Stitch reaches under his bed and takes out a dusty satchel. He pats it down, then puts the book inside. He kneels down by Brown Mouse's cage and opens the door.

"I have to go, Brown Mouse. I might be gone for a long time, so I think it's best that you return to your wanderings in the castle, while I venture out into the world…"

Stitch is filled with a strange fizz of excitement and trepidation.

"… out into the world to look for Henry."

Brown Mouse scoots out of his cage and straight into a crack at the base of the wall.

Stitch watches him go.

He takes one last look at his room, at the marks on the wall. He nods to himself.

He leaves his room and goes into the laboratory. The sunlight shines through the windows in the high ceiling above, illuminating the table that has been ripped from its foundations. It leans over on one side, buckled beyond repair. The connecting wires and tubes have been torn asunder. Glass from broken dials is strewn around the floor. The machines are pitted and scarred as if someone has taken a hammer to them.

Stitch shakes his head in disbelief. "Henry breaks things," he whispers to himself.

Stitch feels light-headed as he approaches the front door, but excited too. He pushes it open.

And for the first time in his life, Stitch properly steps out into the world.

A Terrible Encounter
and a Reunion

The more he walks, the more Stitch feels the "bigness" of the world around him.

"It seems so much larger when you are in it than when you look at it from a distance," he says to himself.

The trees that were once so far away are so near now and so much larger. They tower over him. He spies flowers he has never seen before, a plethora of whites, blues, yellows and reds. He sees bees and other insects. He even sees what Henry often refers to as a "flutterby", its wings white with crimson spots. At one point he spies a bird with a glossy speckled chest, its song a chirping bubbling stream of notes and clicks and whistles. Stitch drinks these sights in. His smile is so broad he feels it might snap, but he keeps smiling and the world keeps getting bigger. It is glorious.

He has walked some distance down the mountain when he realizes he has no idea where he's going.

He felt extremely resolute just after walking out the door, but as he has progressed, his confidence has become a little shaky. He sits cross-legged by the road and takes the book out of his satchel. He thought that bringing the book might inspire him somehow, but now that he's looking at it, he realizes that not being able to read is a major impediment to him actually gaining any kind of inspiration.

He sighs to himself. "I suppose not knowing where Henry has gone does not help matters either."

His ruminations are interrupted by the sounds of a horse and carriage making its way up the mountain path. Stitch puts the book away and stands up and waves cheerily at the driver.

It is Mr Vries.

Mr Vries stops a few feet away from him.

"Hello there, Mr Vries, sir," says Stitch.

Mr Vries regards him with some incredulity. It is as if he has never seen the likes of Stitch even though Stitch knows they have met before, if only very briefly.

Stitch approaches him.

"I'm looking for my friend, Henry. Perhaps you've seen him. A big fellow with a mop of hair and a very pleasant manner."

Mr Vries is still looking at him with a kind of dour amazement.

"Maybe you passed him on your travels?" says Stitch, smiling hopefully.

Mr Vries rubs his grizzled chin. "Can't say I have." He looks about, then looks at Stitch with his eyes narrowed. "You alone?"

Stitch nods.

Mr Vries clambers down from his carriage. "Could be I know where your friend has gone."

"Really? Where might that be?"

Mr Vries is rummaging around in a box as he speaks. "Is this friend of yours anything like you?"

"What do you mean?"

Mr Vries takes out a length of rope, then gestures at Stitch with it. "You know, odd-looking, peculiar to the point of near hideousness."

Stitch is offended. "If you mean is he different, then yes, Henry is different in aspect to many people."

"Another freak, then," says Mr Vries, advancing towards him in a manner Stitch finds most unnerving.

Stitch backs away from him. "I would prefer if you didn't refer to my friend in such a way."

"There's a place for freaks that I know of. I reckon your friend's gone there. A carnival of sorts. A proper good sideshow. They've got them a fish-faced boy and one of them bearded ladies. They'd pay a pretty penny for the likes of you."

He grabs Stitch by the lapel. His eyes are yellow and red-rimmed; his breath is foul. He starts to bind the rope around Stitch's wrist.

"They'll pay handsomely for you too, I reckon."

Stitch twists and turns as he tries to wrest himself from the man's grasp. Mr Vries gives a low gurgling laugh.

"No sense in struggling when there's money to be ma—"

He doesn't finish his sentence. Instead, he straightens up as if hit by a bolt of lightning. He reaches for the back of his head.

"What in ... eugh ... nggh..."

Whatever hit him the first time hits him again. Mr Vries spins around, then hits the ground.

Alice is standing before Stitch, wielding a very large stick.

"Alice! You hit him!"

"He deserved it."

"That was most unexpected." Stitch looks at Vries. "Mainly for Mr Vries."

Stitch grins at Alice. "You came after me." Then he frowns. "Do you mean to bring me back to the castle?"

Alice sighs. "No, Stitch. No I don't."

"Then do you mean to help me find Henry?"

"Could you find him on your own?"

"No, I don't think so."

"Come on, then."

Alice throws her stick aside and starts to walk down the path.

"What about Mr Vries?" Stitch calls after her.

"Let him rest for a bit. He looks like he needs it."

Alice leads him into the forest by the side of the road. Stitch notes that she has a pack with her, no doubt containing supplies for their quest for Henry. She points to some branches and bushes, then at the ground.

"Henry came through here."

"How do you know?"

"I know how to track."

Stitch is very impressed. Henry once told him that many of the explorers in *The Great Book of Exploration* knew how to track so that they could hunt for food.

"You could be an explorer too, Alice."

Alice inspects the ground. Stitch watches her with fascination.

"When did you learn to track?"

"I had to learn a lot of things to survive out in the open when I was younger."

"Did you learn how to hit people as well?"

Alice stands up and looks at the way ahead. "No, that just came naturally with experience."

"Have you hit many people?"

"Too many."

"Did they deserve it?"

"Yes."

"Do you enjoy hitting people?"

"Only when they deserve it," says Alice, glowering at him.

"Are you thinking about hitting someone now?"

"Yes."

"Are you thinking about hitting me?"

"Maybe."

"Should I stop talking?"

"Yes."

Alice sighs, then manages a wry smile. "I'm sorry, Stitch. I didn't mean that."

"That's all right, Alice. I know I ask too many questions."

Alice suddenly looks troubled, and Stitch notes that she can't seem to look at him, just as she avoided looking at him back in the laboratory.

"I'm sorry too that I told Professor Hardacre about White Rabbit. It wasn't my story to tell," she says. "I think I just wanted him to understand you and who you are – a good person, and a loyal friend.

But maybe I gave him too much credit. I don't know if he really appreciates those kinds of things." Alice sighs. "I wish, for his sake, he understood those kinds of things."

Stitch smiles. He'd felt a peculiar sensation when he'd realized Alice had told his story. He wasn't sure what the feeling was. It was a terrible cold, sinking sensation that stayed with him, but now that feeling is gone as he looks at Alice. Alice his friend. Alice who came looking for him. Alice who apologized. He smiles and rests his hand gently on her arm.

"I understand, Alice. We are friends. Friends tell each other their important stories, friends trust each other, and you are friends with Professor Hardacre."

"After a fashion," says Alice, smiling ruefully.

Alice is now able to look him in the eye and smile. This makes Stitch feel almost as happy as he had been before the dreadful experiment on Henry. He feels as if something that was out of balance has just been set right again.

Something in the Night

They walk on, although there are frequent stops for Stitch to pause and admire the greenness of an occasional leaf or the sudden appearance of a squirrel darting up a tree trunk. Stitch is amazed by the colours of the world and its sights and scents. He is surprised Alice isn't as amazed, but he supposes she is used to the outside world. At one point she grabs his arm and points at something.

A few feet away from them, an animal emerges from the undergrowth. It has four legs, and large tangled bony protuberances emerging from its head like a crown.

"A deer," says Alice.

The deer's ears flicker and it holds its head up very regally, then shakes it, and paws the earth with a hoof. Stitch can't help himself; he takes a step towards it and raises his hand.

"Hello," he says.

The deer takes one look at him, then darts off into the forest. Stitch and Alice grin at each other.

They walk on and the sun sinks in the sky. As it sets, they find a glade to shelter in. Stitch feels a certain disappointment that they can't keep moving to look for Henry, but he realizes Alice tires more easily than he does.

Alice eats some bread and an apple she had stored in the backpack she brought with her. She offers Stitch an apple but Stitch explains that he can't eat. They watch the sun go down together.

"I hope Henry is staying hidden," says Alice.

Stitch thinks about what she's said.

"Mr Vries used the words monster and freak." Stitch looks at his hands. "Do you think people in the outside world will think that Henry and I are monsters, because of the way we look, because of the way we were created?"

Alice looks thoughtful now. "The world outside the castle is not what you'd expect. People have ways of looking at others, especially others who don't fit their idea of what a person should look or act like. Mr Vries is proof enough of that."

"But Henry is a person."

"He is."

"As am I."

"People are cruel," says Alice.

"Not all people though," says Stitch.

"No, just enough."

Stitch looks at his hands again. "We are made from dead things, that's what Henry discovered when he read the Professor's notes. Bits and pieces of other people. And Alice, I've been thinking about it... Can I really be a person if I'm made from other people?"

Alice puts her apple down and stands over him. She grabs Stitch's hands.

"Who am I talking to?" she asks, her eyes fierce.

Stitch looks around, as if expecting someone else to appear. "Why, me of course."

"And you are?"

"Stitch."

"Well then, I'm talking to a person, aren't I?"

Stitch smiles. "I suppose you are."

"It doesn't matter what you're made from, it doesn't matter where you came from, all that matters is that you're a good person. With emphasis on *person*. And Henry is too."

Alice takes two blankets from her backpack. She gives one to Stitch, and they prepare to bed down for the night.

Stitch watches the stars come out between the gaps of the overhanging branches and leaves. There are so many of them. He tries to count them all but quickly loses track. He is amazed by their glittering beauty. He even sees a shooting star, its tail glimmering and white for a moment before vanishing into darkness.

"What will you do when we find him?" asks Alice.

Stitch considers her question. He hadn't really thought about it.

"I suppose we could go back to the castle," he says.

Alice gives him a hard look. "Why?"

"Because ... because the castle is our home."

"A home is a place without cruelty, Stitch. The castle is no longer your home, not as long as Professor Hardacre lives there."

Stitch hasn't considered any of this. He sees the truth in what Alice says, but he also can't deny that the castle is all he and Henry have ever known. It's something he decides he will ponder at length.

"Even though he has done bad things I feel sort of sorry for Professor Hardacre. I know you do, Alice."

Alice has already pulled the blanket up over her head and made herself small against the bole of a tree.

Stitch gazes up at the night sky again, contemplating its magnificence.

"The world is big, isn't it, Alice?"

Alice gives a tired muffled response from beneath her blanket.

"I would like to see more of it," says Stitch.

Stitch is woken in the night by someone tapping his arm and clamping a hand over his mouth. He panics for a moment but is relieved to see that it's only Alice. She puts a finger to her lips and signals for him to follow her.

Stitch gets up. He can hear something moving in the trees. He and Alice run and duck for cover

behind some bushes. They wait, holding their breath. Something huge and shambling passes by, blotting out the moon. Its breathing is heavy and laboured and it stands a few feet away from them, sniffing the air, grumbling to itself.

Henry, thinks Stitch. He is just about to break cover and run to Henry but Alice pulls him back, shaking her head violently. Stitch is confused.

The lumbering shadow moves on, and as it does the moon glints off something vivid and blue: a single eye blazing through the night.

Stitch mouths *"The Hooded Man"* to Alice. Now he understands. Alice taps her lips again and they wait until the Hooded Man has moved on into the forest.

When they think it's safe to do so, they head on into the night, neither of them speaking.

A few moments later an agonized Stitch realizes he has left his satchel and *The Great Book of Exploration* behind.

Morning dawns sunny, bright and cool. Stitch watches Alice as they make their way through the trees. She frowns quite a lot, and her eyes seem like they could burrow right into the earth, such is her fierce concentration. She is so absorbed in what she's doing that Stitch is almost afraid to even speak to her.

They make their way out of a patch of the forest and find themselves by a river. Stitch has never seen so much water before. Only pictures in *The Great Book of Exploration*. Thinking about the book again and realizing that he has lost it for ever makes his chest ache.

Stitch sighs, but he is not despondent for long, because the river's magnificence holds him spellbound. He is roused by the pressure of Alice's hand squeezing his arm.

"We must hurry," she says, looking fearfully over his shoulder.

They move on, with Alice increasing her speed. Stitch keeps looking back, and at one point his heart starts to beat that little bit faster as he thinks he catches a flash of movement in the trees behind them.

"Alice?" he says, but Alice only beckons him on.

The vegetation to their right gives way to a steep rocky slope, stubbled with grass and wild flowers. Stitch can't help but look at the flowers, a myriad of purples and reds and yellows. He notices too how the river has broadened, and it flows with a speed that Stitch would never think possible if he didn't see it with his own eyes. The sight is breathtaking. It has gone from a languid smooth flowing motion to a rumbling chundering bellow. Stitch notes how it swirls and slaps against itself; how the water is now tipped with waves of foam; how it glitters under the sun with a new ferocity.

Alice motions for him to stop. She is breathing hard and fast. There is a slightly panicked look in her eyes. She looks at the river, then at the steep slope, then the path forward. She shakes her head.

"He's too close," she says. She points at the slope. "There's cover up there. Come on, climb."

Before Stitch can protest, she is pulling him by the arm and they start to walk up the slope. It is steep and slippery, and Stitch finds it difficult to find purchase at various points, but Alice seems very practised at climbing, and she pulls him along.

They find shelter behind a rock and sit with their backs to it. Alice is panting hard, trying to calm her breathing. She squeezes Stitch's hand.

"Quiet," she whispers.

They stay like that for what seems a long time. All they can hear is the grumble of the river and the chittering of birdsong. Stitch's heart starts to slow; he is almost enjoying the beauty that surrounds them.

Then something snaps down below. A twig perhaps. Stitch holds his breath.

Alice squeezes his hand. Her eyes are wide as they meet his.

Stitch strains to hear. It sounds like something is moving around down below them. He tightens his own grip on Alice's hand.

There is nothing to be heard now. Just birdsong and water and wind.

Stitch exhales slowly. He allows himself a few moments of stillness as he keeps listening. Eventually he starts to lean towards Alice, but the small movement of his shoe dislodges a stone, and that stone hits another, and another, and there is the smallest avalanche of gravel and stone sent trickling down the slope. So small it is barely noticeable by someone who is not paying attention.

But someone is paying attention.

Stitch hears the sound of a boot on stone. A grunt.
More boot steps. Coming closer.

Someone is climbing towards them.

"Run!" shouts Alice.

A Fearful Moment,
and Stitch Steps Up

They launch themselves up from the rock, but Stitch makes a fatal error.

He looks down to see the Hooded Man heading up the slope towards them.

The sight distracts him and Stitch loses his footing. He pinwheels his arms to regain his balance, but it's too late.

Stitch tumbles down the slope.

The world becomes a topsy-turvy blur of stone and sky and flowers. Stitch bounces down the slope. Only one object slows his descent.

The Hooded Man.

He hits him with such force that the Hooded Man is knocked off his feet. He gives a bellow of rage as he tries to scramble up. Stitch is back on his feet, dizzy and sore. The Hooded Man swipes at him but Stitch ducks. He gets a glimpse of the bow and arrow strapped to the Hooded Man's back, and the axe cinched to his belt.

Stitch can only retreat towards the river because now the Hooded Man is between him and the path. The Hooded Man advances towards him; Stitch keeps backing away, closer and closer towards the roar of the water.

The Hooded Man is almost upon him. Stitch is at the very edge of the riverbank, the soil is mucky and soft, and he can feel his feet starting to lose their grip. The Hooded Man reaches for him.

Stitch hears Alice roar in defiance and sees her hurtle towards the Hooded Man. The Hooded Man turns, but this means he is slightly off balance. Alice pushes him, and Stitch has barely time to step aside as the Hooded Man tumbles into the river.

Alice almost falls in after him, but Stitch has enough wits about him to fling his arm out to grab her and stop her momentum. They both collapse in a heap on the ground. Alice pulls Stitch to his feet.

"Quickly!" she shouts. They both head back towards the slope.

But something makes Stitch stop and turn around.

The Hooded Man is splashing desperately in the river, trying to swim back towards the bank, but the current is too strong. He ploughs forward for just a moment, then the river grabs him and he is dragged away.

Stitch takes one look at a bemused Alice. Then he starts to run along the bank, following the Hooded Man.

The Hooded Man is being pulled straight down the river. His head bobs up and down as he gasps for air. The water pulls and drags him, sometimes twirling him around in full circles. Stitch is only vaguely aware that Alice is shouting his name, but he can't take his eyes off the Hooded Man for fear of losing sight of him.

The Hooded Man is momentarily dashed against a rocky outcrop. He scrabbles in panic at the edge of it, manages to cling on.

Stitch runs towards him across his side of the bank. Alice is screaming at him now. He can hear her running behind him.

The Hooded Man loses his grip, flails at water and thin air, and is spun out into the river again. He dips under the surface and Stitch cannot see him any more.

Stitch spots a log perched on the bank. He runs to it and tries to push it into the river. Alice is upon him now.

"What are you doing?" she shouts above the roar of the river.

Stitch sees that the Hooded Man has resurfaced and is holding on to a rock in the centre of the river, but he is clearly getting weaker.

"He can't hold on for much longer! Help me push!" he shouts at Alice.

Alice shakes her head for just a moment, then she throws herself at the log just as Stitch does, and it splashes into the water.

They watch as it is caught like a twig in the watery maelstrom. The Hooded Man slips from the rock. The log is being tossed by the current.

The Hooded Man loses his grip and is sent careering down the river.

But the log is spinning towards him.

Stitch watches, heart pounding so hard he can feel it in his mouth.

The log is spinning past the Hooded Man.

Somehow he lunges at it...

The Hooded Man grabs hold of the log.

"Yes!" Stitch shouts, clapping his hands with delight.

He and Alice watch as the Hooded Man holds on to the log, the current taking him towards the grassy bank on the other side. He crashes into the bank and manages to gain some purchase on the grass and halt the log's movement.

He is some distance away now, but Stitch can see the Hooded Man gather his strength. He clambers from the log on to the bank, and then lies there, panting with exhaustion.

"Come on," says Alice, taking Stitch's hand.

They head back the way they came. Stitch allows himself one last look at the Hooded Man, who is now standing and looking across the water at him.

"Why did you help him?"

Stitch shrugs. "You helped too, Alice."

Alice looks pensive. "It was a strange thing to do."

"It was the right thing to do."

Alice looks at him for a moment. Stitch smiles at her.

"You know it was, Alice. You know it because you are—"

"A good person. So you keep saying, Stitch. Not all people are good."

Stitch's smile broadens. "No, not all. But enough."

A Place Without Monsters

As they leave the river behind, they push on through the forest and the trees become more densely packed. The light that surrounds them now is green and liquid and soft. Stitch marvels at its quality. He feels like running his fingers through it like water.

Alice stops for a moment and raises her hand.

"Do you smell that?" she says.

Stitch sniffs the air. "Smoke," he says.

There is no mistaking it: a burning earthy smell that seems somehow comforting. A smell that reminds him of the log fires the Professor was so fond of in the castle. Both he and Alice look upwards, and through a gap in the branches they see a light column of smoke spiralling lazily up to the sky. There is something else too.

Someone is groaning, as if in pain. Stitch and Alice exchange puzzled looks. They move forward slowly.

They peer through the trees to see a small, whitewashed cottage surrounded by greenery and wild flowers. Smoke is coming from the chimney, and the front door is a dark blue. Everything about the cottage and its surroundings looks wonderfully inviting to Stitch.

The moans of pain are closer now. "Look, Alice," says Stitch, pointing.

An old man lies on the ground in front of the cottage. There is a stick by his side. Stitch looks at Alice. She shakes her head, but Stitch is already moving towards the man.

"Hello," says Stitch.

"Who's that? Who's there?" asks the old man, looking around in panic. His eyes are filmy and grey. With a pang of sadness, Stitch realizes the old man is blind.

"I'm sorry, I didn't mean to startle you," says Stitch. "Let us help you."

Both Stitch and Alice help the man to his feet.

"I fell," says the man. "I think I hurt my ankle."

Stitch and Alice bear his weight and help him inside the cottage. They deposit him gently in a chair by the fire. The fire gives the interior a lovely warm glow. Stitch sees a narrow bed over by the window on the right, and to the left of the fire is a wooden table with a couple of rickety chairs.

"Thank you, thank you," says the man, patting Stitch on the arm.

"You are most welcome. My name is Stitch, and this is my friend, Alice."

Alice grabs a small stool and she places the old man's leg on it and examines his ankle.

"I'm very pleased, indeed fortunate, to meet you," says the man, with a quivery smile. "My name is Samuel."

"I can strap this up. You should rest," says Alice.

Samuel directs her to a cupboard, where Alice finds some bandages. She is very brisk but gentle as she straps his ankle. Stitch winces when he sees the bruising.

"Have you anyone who can help you, Samuel?" asks Stitch.

Samuel shakes his head. "Only my daughter and her husband, but they haven't been for weeks."

"I'll make something to eat," says Alice.

Alice goes through Samuel's cupboards and finds some vegetables. Stitch watches in amazement as she makes some soup. Meanwhile he sits with Samuel and listens to his stories of how he has lived here since he was a boy. Stitch likes Samuel. He reminds him of the Professor with his bushy white eyebrows and his beard.

Alice serves up the soup at the table, being mindful of two things. One, to bring Samuel's soup to him as he sits by the fire, and two, to pretend to pour soup into a bowl for Stitch. Stitch feels guilty about this as he watches Samuel eat his soup.

"You won't be able to put any weight on that for at least a few days," says Alice.

"I can manage," says Samuel.

Alice shakes her head. "No you can't. You'll need someone to help you."

Samuel looks crestfallen. "There's no one."

"What about your daughter and her husband?" asks Stitch.

Samuel sighs. "They're not very dependable."

Samuel trails off, looking sorrowful. Stitch looks at Alice. Alice nods.

"We'll help you," says Alice.

Stitch is torn. On the one hand he wants to help Samuel, but on the other he still wants to find Henry. But he looks at Samuel sitting in his chair, trembling slightly, and he knows there is only one thing to do.

"Alice is right. We will help you," says Stitch.

They talk some more and before they know it, night is drawing in. Alice and Stitch help Samuel to bed. Alice makes up two beds from straw in the shed beside Samuel's cottage, and she and Stitch settle down for the night.

Stitch can't sleep. He is still in two minds.

"We need to find Henry," he says.

"Yes," says Alice, her voice sounding muffled in the dark.

"But we can't leave Samuel."

"No."

"Then we should stay for a while, and make sure Samuel is all right because it would be the right thing to do, and you should always do the right thing for the right reasons. The Professor told me that."

Alice moves in the dark. She appears to be sitting up.

"What was he like?"

"He was good, and kind. He taught us to be good and kind also. He brought me and Henry into the world, so I suppose he was very generous in his way too."

"How so?"

"Well, to create someone, to give them life, is a very generous thing."

"I suppose," says Alice, lying back down.

Stitch lies down too. He thinks about all the sights he has seen; he thinks about the world and how much more of it there must be. He thinks about Henry.

"We will find him, won't we, Alice?"

"We will, I promise."

And that is enough for Stitch.

Over the next two days Samuel tries to convince them to leave, but Alice insists that they stay until his ankle is fully healed. Samuel seems glad of the company, and they prepare his meals for him and do his chores. Alice frequently catches Stitch's eye and tells him to stop worrying about Henry. Stitch tries his best, but he can't get Henry out of his mind, and he can't help thinking how big the world is and how Henry, for all his size, will feel lost in it.

On the second night, Samuel tells them stories of his youth. He is particularly fond of ghost stories and tales of strange happenings. He says he has one story that is "especially grisly".

"What's that now?" asks Stitch.

"There is a tale told of a man of science who lives in a castle not far from here," says Samuel.

The hair on the back of Stitch's neck starts to prickle, and he and Alice exchange a look with each other.

"A man of science?" asks Alice.

"So he has called himself for many years. Rumour has it that he has performed horrific experiments – experiments that are akin to sorcery. He is in league with a brutish type, a man who robs graves, and it is said this man of science uses dead bodies to create monsters."

Samuel nods in satisfaction and smiles at the gruesomeness of his tale, but no one else is smiling. A disconsolate Stitch is looking at the floor. Alice gazes into the fire.

"Has anyone ever seen these monsters?" asks Stitch.

"There have been sightings – strange creatures glimpsed in the forest at night, howling at the moon."

Stitch looks at Alice and mouths "*Henry*".

"It sounds like a slightly unbelievabubb— I mean, unbelievable story," says Stitch.

Samuel looks thoughtful. "Perhaps, but rumours start from somewhere and have a habit of gaining a life of their own." He frowns. "And there have been so many stories."

"Perhaps these stories have a grain of truth," says Alice. "There are different kinds of monsters; some are not so obvious as others. A man might look like the most civil, well-behaved person when meeting strangers for the first time, but in secret he may be monstrous in his own fashion."

Samuel smiles. "You seem to be wise beyond your years, Alice."

"She is, she is very wise. I'm always telling her," says Stitch eagerly.

Samuel beckons them both forward. "Come here so that I can see you both."

Stitch is bemused by this, and so is Alice, but they move nearer to Samuel.

"Come closer," says Samuel to Alice.

He reaches up with both hands and clasps Alice's face. He smiles. "So, this is you, Alice. I'm pleased to make your acquaintance."

He turns to Stitch.

"And Stitch?"

Stitch shakes his head, and edges away from him. "I don't … I…"

Samuel is smiling, and once again Stitch feels guilty about his deception. He steps closer and leans down. Samuel takes his face in both hands.

"And this is you, Stitch."

Stitch feels like the moment is lasting for ever. Samuel smiles. Alice nods encouragingly at Stitch. Samuel takes his hands away from Stitch's face, and Stitch relaxes. But then Samuel takes both of Stitch's hands in his, and for just a moment he frowns.

Stitch quickly pulls his hands away.

Samuel looks confused.

"I was thinking perhaps I should do the washing up before bed. It is getting late," says Stitch.

"Of course," says Samuel.

Stitch turns away from Samuel, but then something strikes him.

"Samuel, there is something of utmost importance I must share with you."

Alice looks concerned. She shakes her head at him.

Samuel looks troubled by Stitch's tone. "What is it, Stitch?"

Stitch swallows hard before he says, "I want you to know something, something very important. You spoke of monsters, and I want you to know..."

Alice takes a step towards him and mouths "*No*", but Stitch is resolute in what he wants to say.

"There are no monsters here, Samuel. Only very dear friends," says Stitch.

He takes Samuel's hand in his.

Alice exhales with relief and smiles.

Samuel pats Stitch's hand. "Of course, I know that, Stitch. And you're both most welcome."

"No monsters, only friends," says Stitch.

Stitch goes to bed that night feeling good about himself. He and Alice have done something important, he thinks. He has made a new friend in the outside world, and in his own fashion that new friend has seen him and accepted him. He feels sad knowing that they will be leaving Samuel very soon to look for Henry, but he knows the comfort of them both being friends will soften things

He looks up at the ceiling, thinking back on his adventure so far. It has all been very interesting and exciting, but just before he goes to sleep he thinks about the most important thing of all. He thinks about Henry. He misses him terribly. He hopes that he is safe and that he will see him very soon.

A Most Dreadful Day

On the day everything changes, Stitch and Alice are out gathering berries.

Alice is humming as she picks. Stitch stops what he is doing and marvels at this. Alice becomes aware that he is looking at her.

"What?" she says.

"Alice, you are happy."

Stitch is instantly sorry he said anything because Alice looks very fiercely at him.

"Have I said something wrong?"

"You sounded surprised."

"Because you are happy, and I don't think I've ever seen you happy."

Alice looks taken aback. "I can be happy."

"Clearly."

"I can be happy any time I want to be," she says defensively.

"I don't doubt it. It's just that I've never seen you happy until now."

Alice seems to mull this over. She returns to picking berries. Stitch watches her out of the corner of his eye. She stops what she's doing for a moment, and without looking at him says, "I was happy sometimes, when I was small. Happy with the other children in the orphanage. I was even happy helping them on the street when the orphanage was closed, making sure they were all right before we all went our separate ways. But when I think about it now, I don't suppose it was proper happiness I was feeling. Not really."

"Until now?"

Alice looks at him. She smiles, grudgingly, in the way Stitch has become accustomed to.

"Until now," she says.

"Because now you have friends."

"Yes."

And now her smile isn't so grudging.

They continue picking berries and Stitch has a feeling of ease and contentment.

Stitch's basket is full and he decides to go back to the cottage while Alice continues looking for berries. He swings his basket and hums to himself as he makes his way back through the trees. Everything is so leafy green and drenched in sunlight, and Stitch still finds each day a marvel out here in the wide world.

He is so taken up by the greenness of things around him that he doesn't really notice the woman as he steps out from the trees. It's only when she screams that he realizes she's there.

Stitch is so startled, he drops his basket.

The woman is pointing at him and shrieking, "Monster! Monster!"

Stitch holds his hands out to placate her, but this only seems to make her worse. He sees a man sprint from the cottage. He is followed by Samuel, who limps out with the help of his stick.

"What's wrong? What's happening?" asks Samuel.

The man grabs a rake and heads straight for Stitch. The woman is still screaming.

Stitch feels a hand squeeze his arm so hard it almost hurts. He turns to see Alice by his side. Her face is white, her eyes filled with terror.

"Run!" she shouts.

They run back into the trees. Stitch takes a moment to look back and sees the woman go to Samuel, who is shaking his head and remonstrating with her. The man wielding the rake is still chasing after them, thrashing tree branches aside. Alice hauls Stitch after her. She makes a series of twists and turns so elaborate that they make Stitch dizzy, but her tactic means they are soon out of the man's sight.

Stitch falls; the earth smacks into his face. He is dazed, and one side of his face feels numb. Alice drags him up. They keep running, tree branches slapping against them, bushes and brambles tearing at them. Stitch stumbles, Alice rights him. He tries to speak.

"Alice … what…?"

She just shakes her head and drags him on with a grim determination.

They finally stop running after what seems like an age. Both of them gasping for breath, looking around to make sure nobody is following them. The trees here are tightly packed, hemming them in.

Stitch bends over and tries to catch his breath. Alice leans against a tree. Stitch notices red weals on her face where the branches have struck her. He touches his own face, but he feels nothing; nothing except an awful burning sensation deep in his very being. A strange mixture of despondency and shame.

"What *happened*?" he finally manages to say.

Alice waves her hand weakly back in the direction they came from. "Must be Samuel's daughter and husband ... probably bringing supplies. Of all times ... they decide to..."

Stitch sits down, but Alice grabs him by the elbow and drags him up.

"We have to keep going," says Alice.

"Why?" asks Stitch.

"Because they'll be coming," says Alice.

They walk through the day, and on through the night. It's a night that brings rain. Heavy rain that soaks them to their very bones, but they keep moving in search of shelter. At one point they pass the village and Stitch looks forlornly at the warm orange glow of dozens of lights. Everything about it seems safe and homely, and it just makes him feel more wretched.

He thinks about the castle and Professor Hardacre, but he fights the urge to mention it. He fears that if he does say it out loud, Alice will be angry. The night is cold and wet, and the world is now an unfriendly place.

Stitch looks at Alice with her wet hair plastered to her face. She seems exhausted and broken. Alice who is so often resolute and determined and brave.

They walk on into the dark.

Something Very Unexpected Indeed

"I haven't been marking my days."

They've taken a rest in a part of the forest huddled against the side of a mountain. The rain has eased to a soft mizzle the trees and mountain providing some protection against it. The moon offers some light through a break in the clouds. Stitch has been thinking about everything that has happened to them. He now realizes some of the things that he's missed.

"What's that?" asks Alice, sitting on a rock.

"My days. The days I've been in the world. I used to mark them," says Stitch. "But ever since..." He trails off.

"Why did you do that, Stitch?"

Stitch shrugs. "I don't know. I liked to do it. I like being in the world, and every day is different."

"Today is certainly different," says Alice.

She stands up and points at the mountain. "We can go around it, or we can climb."

"Or we could just stay here," says Stitch. "It's very dark. The dark is a good place to hide."

Alice shakes her head. She looks determined. Stitch knows that look. He feels encouraged to see it returning.

"They'll be coming for us," she says. "We need to keep moving."

But when do we stop? thinks Stitch. *Can we ever stop?* he wonders.

"And we still need to find Henry," he says.

Alice nods. "Escape first, then find Henry. We can do both. We *will* do both," she says.

They trudge on through the forest. Stitch is grateful for the breeze that dries their clothes and the fact that there's no more rain.

The moon vanishes behind a cloud, and now Stitch can't help but feel an ominous sense that something bad is going to happen. That feeling is only heightened when Alice glances over her shoulder and he sees her look of surprise.

Stitch turns to see orange lights blinking in and out in the undergrowth, some distance behind them. They appear and disappear at random intervals, but they seem to be getting closer.

"Flames," says Alice.

"From torches," says Stitch, as he realizes what is happening. "Samuel's daughter must have raised the alarm."

The villagers are coming for them. Alice grabs Stitch by the shoulder and drags him on.

They rush on blindly through the dark. The darkness becomes deeper, more oppressive. Eventually Alice is only a vague outline in the gloom. The only sounds are their laboured breathing. Stitch feels as if he is in a slow-moving waking nightmare. He hears sounds now. People talking amongst themselves. The voices are getting closer. Then he hears the shouts.

"There they are!"

Stitch can smell smoke now. The flames of the

torches glide and bob through the trees and with them a horde of shouting silhouettes.

The forest before Stitch and Alice becomes an ugly shifting canvas of flickering flame and shadow. Horrid screams follow in their wake as they keep running. Shouts of "Get them!"

There is a ravine to their right; it leads down into darkness. Stitch turns to look at the seething mass of shadows, faces occasionally lit up by their torches. Faces that are a mixture of panic and anger. He recognizes Mr Vries among them, his face twisted with hate. Stitch turns back, but his foot catches on something. He has just enough time to see the look of horror on Alice's face.

"Stitch!" she screams.

Stitch feels his feet go out from under him. The world flips over and over as Stitch tumbles into darkness.

The first thing Stitch is aware of is the smell of smoke and the flicker of flame.

He finds he is staring up at a wooden raftered ceiling rather than the night sky. This confuses him.

Everything spins for just a moment, so Stitch closes his eyes tight until he feels still. He can hear someone mumbling. He turns his head and opens his eyes.

His eyesight is a little blurry, but he can just make out a huge hulking figure sitting by a fire. The figure seems to be talking to himself.

Stitch's voice is only a croak, but he manages a weak "Hello."

The figure jumps up in fright. He is gradually coming into focus. Stitch can now see his bulky shoulders, his huge hands.

That unmistakable blue eye.

Stitch's heart pounds as he realizes he has been captured by the Hooded Man.

Stitch discovers he's in a bed. He tries to wrestle himself out from under the blanket. The Hooded Man steps forward, a hand outstretched.

"No. Rest."

Stitch tries to rise again, but he stops suddenly when he notices something.

The Hooded Man's hand is grey and leathery. Stitch looks beyond his arm to where his huge domed head sits on his impossibly broad shoulders. He sees the one vivid eye, and the other eye which has been stitched shut. He sees the grey skin and the zigzag traces of stitches that cover his face. Stitch gasps.

"You're just like me and Henry."

The Hooded Man turns his face away. "Must rest."

Stitch isn't listening to his instruction. He's too fascinated now. He manages to move into a sitting position by the side of the bed. His eyes rove over the interior of the small cabin. The walls are earthen. There is a small table and one other chair.

"I'm Stitch, what's your name?"

The Hooded Man can't look at Stitch. He waves a hand dismissively.

"Stitch, rest."

"What's your name?"

The Hooded Man reluctantly looks at him. Eventually he taps his chest. "Gregor."

"Gregor. Well now, I'm very pleased to meet you, Gregor." Then, with startling clarity, Stitch realizes something else.

"You came first!"

Gregor looks uncomfortable with this statement.

"We always thought it was Henry, but you must have been there all along..." Stitch's train of thought is interrupted by another thought. "Why did you save me?"

Gregor looks at him, his forehead wrinkling. "Stitch save Gregor, so Gregor save Stitch."

He sits his vast bulk down on one of the chairs and looks at the fire. "Stitch rest now."

Stitch gets out of the bed feeling a little woozy, but also excited by this new discovery.

"Why didn't you stay in the castle with the old Professor after he woke you?"

Gregor shakes his head, refusing to answer.

"Did something happen?"

Gregor looks at the floor.

"Were you sent away?"

Gregor bellows. "Gregor leave coz Gregor wanted to. Gregor decide. Not Professor. Gregor!"

Surprisingly, Stitch doesn't feel threatened by this outburst. He approaches Gregor slowly. Gregor has his head in his hands.

"You didn't like it there?"

Gregor sits up straight. He looks towards the window.

"All wrong. Gregor not like. Gregor left, but still Professor made Gregor bring things, machine things, wood things. Dead things. And still Professor make new people, and Gregor not like that because…"

"Did it seem wrong to you?"

Gregor nods.

"Do you know why?"

Gregor shakes his head.

"I see," says Stitch. "It's a strange thing to create new life from…" Stitch looks at his hands.

Gregor nods again. "Dead things. People."

"You could have just left altogether."

Gregor runs a hand over his head. "Gregor find it hard say no, because Gregor … because … Professor…"

"Because he made you?"

Gregor sighs.

Stitch sits in the chair next to Gregor's. Gregor laces his fingers together and looks at them. They say nothing for a moment. The fire crackles.

"Did Professor Hardacre send you after us?"

Gregor nods. Stitch notices he looks guilty.

"Young Professor send Gregor after Stitch and Small Man and girl."

"Small Man?"

Gregor stands up; he waggles his head and shoulders back and forth, wiggles his fingers against each other, and says in a silly voice, "What do now, Stitch? Me have bibbledy bobbledy head. Me like moon. Oh moon kissy kissy moon."

Gregor sits back down.

Stitch grins. "Henry. You mean Henry."

Gregor nods. "Small Man."

"Small?" Stitch lets out a sudden burst of laughter at the absurdity of this, then Gregor starts to laugh. Before he knows it, Stitch has tears running down his face from uncontrollable laughter while Gregor's shoulders go up and down and he gurgles "Ah har har, ah har har!" over and over in his deep rumbling voice.

Stitch wipes the tears of laughter from his eyes. "Oh, that was amusing."

Gregor smirks. "Small Man is funny. Talks too much, but funny." Gregor's face darkens. "Gregor didn't like what Young Professor was doing to Small Man."

"Neither did I," says Stitch. And now he realizes something else. "Gregor, did you destroy the laboratory because of what Professor Hardacre was trying to do to Henry?"

Gregor nods.

"I see. It all makes sense. Does Professor Hardacre know you destroyed the laboratory?"

Gregor shakes his head.

Stitch is intrigued. "But you still took orders from him. You still came after us. Why?"

Gregor sighs. "Gregor not do it for new Professor. Bad world outside. Gregor not sure Stitch and Small Man should be in it. Bad world. Safer in castle. Safer now machine broken."

"You were concerned for us!" says Stitch, smiling broadly. Gregor looks slightly embarrassed by this revelation.

Stitch spots a book on the table – *The Great Book of Exploration*!

"You found it! You found my book!"

Stitch grabs it and examines it, delighted to discover that it's not damaged.

"Can you read, Gregor?"

"Not read, no."

"We're very much the same, you and I. And Henry too."

Gregor makes a face. "Small Man is smaller than Gregor."

"So you found me and brought me back here. But what happened to Alice?"

"Villagers take girl. Take Small Man too."

"They have Henry?" says Stitch, feeling a mixture of delight and anxiety.

Gregor nods. "Small Man wander into village. Villagers take him."

"Then I must go and find Henry and Alice."

Stitch stomps towards the door, but before he opens it he realizes something. He turns back and looks at Gregor. "Unfortunately, I don't know the way to the village."

Gregor stands up. The top of his head almost brushes the ceiling.

"Gregor knows way. Gregor help Stitch find girl and Small Man."

A Rescue and a Perilous Moment for Henry

As they make their way through the forest, Stitch can feel the old familiar pressure in the air. A storm is approaching. Already he can see the peaks of the mountains fringed with threads of lightning, followed by the distant low rumble of thunder.

"Storm," says Gregor. "Gregor not like storms."

Stitch pats him on the arm. "It'll be all right, Gregor."

By the time they reach the outskirts of the village the thunder is much louder and the lightning is creeping closer. Gregor points.

"There."

Stitch follows the line of his finger to a large barn.

"Villagers put Small Man in there. Gregor see. Girl too maybe."

Stitch steps forward, but Gregor grabs his arm and jerks his head in the direction of the street.

Stitch spots some people milling around at the other end of the main street. The barn is at the far end of town nearer the forest. Stitch realizes if they wait for just the right moment, they can run for cover and hopefully no one will be looking in their direction.

Just then, a flash of lightning bathes the main street in white light. Stitch looks at the crowd gathered at the other end of the street. They appear to be building something.

The street is dark again. Stitch nods, and he and Gregor make a run for the barn. Stitch is silently hoping that another bolt of lightning doesn't reveal them, but the village people seem to be more concerned about what they're building. He and Gregor dash across the main street.

They make it to the barn. The door is tied shut with a length of chain. Stitch's heart sinks.

Gregor moves him gently out of the way. He grabs the chain, and he pulls. The chain links snap easily, as though made of paper. Gregor grins at Stitch's look of amazement.

They push the door open to find Alice rushing towards them with a long wooden pole. Stitch has barely enough time to shout "Alice!", and she's moving so fast that he's not sure she will stop before…

Gregor bats the pole away with ease.

"It's all right, he's a friend, Alice," says Stitch.

Alice looks at Gregor with astonishment. "He's…"

"Just like Henry and me," says Stitch. "Speaking of which…" Stitch looks around him.

"They've taken him, Stitch. The villagers have taken Henry. They say they're going to burn him because he's a monster."

And with a horrible sinking feeling, Stitch now realizes what the villagers have been building. They watch from the shadows just outside the shed. The villagers are indeed gathering wood into a pile for a makeshift pyre. Stitch's thoughts are panicked and wild. *Why would they hurt Henry?*

Gregor sighs "Bad world. See?"

Stitch can't make any sense of what he's seeing, but he knows he must do something about it. He sees Henry with his hands tied behind his back being prodded towards the pole that juts out from the centre of the pyre. Stitch takes a deep breath.

"We will rescue Henry," he says. "But we need a distraction."

Stitch points at the small alleys that run up the length of the main street. "If we can sneak up through the edge of town, we can come out the other end and perhaps grab Henry."

"And the distraction?" asks Alice.

Stitch straightens. "That would be me."

Alice protests furiously when Stitch tells her the detail of his plan. But Stitch has made his decision and will not waver. Alice reluctantly concedes when Stitch says, "Look at me, Alice. I am much more of a distraction than you could ever be."

Stitch watches Alice and Gregor creep away through the dark. Alice gives him one last stern look, but Stitch smiles encouragingly at her.

Stitch makes his way up the street. He takes deep breaths, and his heart, which has been pounding ever since they arrived at the village, starts to slow.

The crowd is being urged on by Mr Vries. He is carrying a torch larger than the others, and his behaviour reminds him of Professor Hardacre's bitterness and rage. Henry is being tied to the pole by two men. Stitch is so close to the crowd now that he can smell the oily smokiness of their torches. He raises himself up to his full height.

The plan is to distract the crowd for long enough so that Alice and Gregor might free Henry. The plan is for Stitch to perhaps lure the crowd away to enable this to happen.

The plan is for him to run.

But suddenly and astoundingly, even to him, Stitch decides he doesn't want to run. Stitch realizes that he is no longer afraid. He walks out in front of the crowd.

"Hello there," he begins.

Stitch Speaks

The townsfolk turn to see him just as forked lightning rips across the sky. Some of the people gasp, others point. They all look horrified, but Stitch carries on with his cheery demeanour.

"My name is Stitch. I see you have my friend Henry. I was wondering if you might consider letting him go."

Mr Vries is snarling, his stubbled jowls greasy in the torchlight.

"Another one of the monsters. The one that deceived Samuel! Take him!"

Some of the crowd start to move forward, but Stitch raises his hands just as lightning flashes overhead once more. This seems to halt the crowd in their tracks. It also allows Stitch to see some of their faces more clearly. He spies Samuel's daughter and her husband. He waves at them.

"Hello Samuel's daughter and husband. It is very nice to see you again."

Samuel's daughter's face is contorted in a grimace, as is her husband's. Samuel's daughter has a cudgel raised in her hand. Stitch recognizes their expressions for what they truly are: not of hate, but of fear.

"I must say it was very nice staying with Samuel. He made me and Alice feel very at home."

"You tricked him!" says Samuel's daughter.

"How?" asks Stitch. He is surprised by how calm he feels in the face of the crowd. He notices two shadows sidling up to Henry in the dark. Both shadows, one large and one small, start untying Henry. The men who have originally tied Henry to the post seem to be just as distracted by Stitch as the rest of the crowd.

"He didn't know you were a monster," says Samuel's son-in-law.

"And in what way am I monstrous?" asks Stitch.

Both Samuel's daughter and her husband look

suddenly unsure of themselves. Samuel's daughter points her cudgel at him.

"By ... by looking like that," she says.

Stitch looks at his hands and smiles. "That would seem to me to be an unfair accusation considering that none of us present are responsible for how we look," says Stitch. He points at a man in the crowd. "There is a gentleman there with one ear larger than the other. Surely no one would hold such a thing against him." The man he points at touches his ear self-consciously and looks embarrassed. "I see another gentleman whose hair is rather sparse, and yet it is not something I would judge him for."

Someone guffaws in the crowd, and the balding man Stitch pointed to glares in the direction of the laughter.

Stitch turns his attention back to Samuel's daughter. "Also, when Alice and I met him, Samuel was injured and we helped him. Did he mention any wicked acts on my part?"

Samuel's daughter and her husband exchange a look.

"Your deception was enough," shouts Samuel's son-in-law. Samuel's daughter puts a hand on his arm to quieten him.

"There was no deception on my part or Alice's. We simply helped a friend. Samuel would tell you so."

"My father said you cooked his meals," says Samuel's daughter, eyeing Stitch warily.

"Because we did," says Stitch, mildly. "And we picked berries for him and made sure he was comfortable."

"Ignore the creature; he is clearly not to be trusted," snarls Mr Vries.

"And are you to be trusted, Mr Vries? Especially considering your intention was to sell me to what you term a 'freak show' when last we met?"

Mr Vries looks shaken. He tries to scoff at Stitch's comment. "Pay him no heed, the monster lies. It's in his nature."

Some of the crowd murmur to each other now, and to Stitch they all look a little more uncertain of themselves. The air feels less charged with anger and electricity; the lightning has receded, and the thunder rumbles far away. Stitch is also happy to see that Alice and Gregor have almost completely untied Henry. Stitch turns his focus back to the crowd. He looks as many of them in the eye as he can. Some look frightened, some angry, and yet some also look curious. Stitch takes a deep breath.

"I don't know much about the world, having been in it only a matter of nearly six hundred days or thereabouts, but I have noticed that some people use words such as 'monster' and 'freak' when they encounter someone they perceive to be different. But as I told a friend of mine once, everybody is different, and this is what makes the world such a curious and interesting place. I don't believe hurting someone just because you think they are different is a course of action anyone should take. In the particular case of Henry, I think it is even more peculiar and unwelcome, especially so because Henry is a good person, and he is my friend."

"Pah, *person*," splutters an agitated Mr Vries.

"Yes, person. The world is large and wonderful and multifarious. There is room enough for everyone, even for those like Henry and me. I would go as far as to say that we belong in it as much as anyone, no matter what other people might think."

Stitch feels his body sag with relief when he notices that the others have managed to sneak Henry away from the pyre. There are mutterings in the crowd; some people are whispering to each other while eyeing Stitch. Mr Vries swallows hard; he looks panicked.

"Don't just stand there, grab the monster!"

And yet amazingly no one moves. There are more whispers, and some of the crowd are blinking as if seeing Stitch for the first time. Stitch catches some snatches of what they are saying.

"He speaks like a person ... remarkable ... what if what he says is true ... almost like a proper ... reasonable..."

The crowd had been a shifting spikey mass of shadows before Stitch spoke. Now the edges have been smoothed away, they peer inquisitively where once their eyes blazed with fury; they murmur to each other, and their movements are relaxed, less threatening.

Samuel's daughter lowers her cudgel. Her expression has softened. She applies gentle pressure on her husband's arm and silently encourages him to lower his club. He does so. Stitch notices the same kind of expression on the faces of many others: a mixture of curiosity, disbelief, a grudging but definite acceptance.

The threat of the storm has passed, and now all it leaves in its wake is a gentle rain. Stitch puts his head back and feels the rain on his face. "It is good to be out in the world and exploring, even in spite of the weather."

Stitch smiles at the people.

"What are you all doing?" screams Mr Vries. "Grab it. Burn it!"

He pushes some of his companions, prods them, pokes them, he shouts in their faces, but none of them seem willing to do anything. All of them just look at Stitch as if he has somehow transformed into something miraculous.

Then a cry rings out. "The other one has escaped!"

The crowd turn their attention towards the pyre. Stitch takes the opportunity to run. Mr Vries chases after him, but from the way he pants and waddles it is clear to Stitch that he is not a man used to much exertion. In desperation, he hurls his torch at Stitch. Stitch manages to duck out of the way. The torch flies over his head and crashes through the window of a nearby house.

The curtains inside *whoosh* as flames take hold of them. Both Stitch and Mr Vries are shocked enough to stop in their tracks for just a split second. Stitch has enough of his wits about him to start running again, and moments later he finds the others waiting for him just inside the treeline.

"Stitch!" Henry shouts.

He grabs Stitch and raises him up and embraces him with all his might.

"Stitch, oh Stitch," he says, tears of joy springing to his eyes.

"You can put me down now, Henry."

Henry lets him go, then points at Gregor.

"Look, Stitch. The Hooded Man without his hood. He looks just like us!"

"Not like Small Man. Gregor bigger," says Gregor.

A confused Henry looks around. "What small man? I don't see one."

"Ah hur hur, Small Man is funny," Gregor gurgles.

Henry looks confused at first, then hurt when he realizes what Gregor is saying.

"But I'm not... I'm..." he sputters.

"We have to go!" says Stitch.

"The villagers will be coming," says Alice.

And just at that moment there is an explosion of orange in the sky. People start wailing.

"I don't think they'll be paying us much attention. Mr Vries has accidentally set fire to one of their houses," says Stitch.

Gregor ushers them deeper into the forest. A grateful Stitch realizes they are moments away from freedom.

But something stops him in his tracks.

He turns to look up through a gap in the trees. The whole house is ablaze now. He can see dozens of people running back and forth with buckets of water frantically trying to extinguish the blaze, but to no avail. He can hear screaming.

Children screaming.

Stitch looks at the others. Henry frowns at him.

"Stitch?"

The fire

$\int$titch starts to walk back towards the village. He is dimly aware that the others are following him. but his focus is on the house.

"Stitch? What are you doing?" Alice asks.

Stitch is unable to answer. He just knows he has one of his powerful feelings of rightness. He leads everyone out from the forest, back into the village.

He and the others stand before the blazing house. Men, women and children are doing their utmost to extinguish the fire, but it seems to be growing in ferocity. Mr Vries is gibbering by the sidelines. There is a mixture of confusion and panic, and the presence of Stitch and his friends seems to be the least of the townsfolk's worries.

Stitch can hear the screams emanating from the house.

A man and a woman are being dragged away from the fire by others, who are pleading with them not to go back in. They are soot-stained and coughing.

"My children! My children are still in there!" the woman cries.

"How many?" Alice asks a man who is desperately throwing water from a bucket on to the flames.

"Three," he says.

Alice looks at Stitch. There are some men attempting to get into the house, but they are being beaten back by the heat and are unable to enter. *Henry, Gregor and I are different though*, Stitch thinks.

Stitch nods at Henry and Gregor. They instinctively understand his signal and they follow him towards the house and make their way through the crowd. The people are too concerned about the fire to pay them the proper attention. Stitch is grateful for that. He and Henry and Gregor enter the house.

The air is hot inside. Stitch feels it rake his throat, his eyes start streaming, and he coughs. He hears the children screaming. He can already see two cowering behind a dresser. A boy and a small girl. He coaxes them out and Henry takes one under each arm, ignoring their squeals, and rushes out of the house.

"There's one more," Stitch shouts at Gregor.

He hears a girl screaming up above.

He points. "Upstairs!"

Gregor dashes in front of him. He is almost at the top, and Stitch is only halfway up, when a flaming rafter collapses from the ceiling and falls on the stairs, destroying the top steps in the process. Stitch reels backwards just in time. He sees Gregor on the balcony.

"Find her!" Stitch shouts, in an effort to be heard over the roaring flames.

Gregor disappears from view. Stitch can feel the encroaching heat on his skin now. It's as he suspected. He is more resistant to the deadly effects of the fire than others. *But not for long*, he thinks, as his throat tightens in pain, and his hair almost sizzles.

He begins to think he won't see Gregor again.

Then out of the smoke and flame Gregor reappears with a tiny girl cradled in his arms.

Stitch looks at the flaming remains of the stairs. There is only one thing for it.

"Throw her to me," he shouts.

He stands under the balcony, praying that there is enough time. Gregor launches the girl into the air.

She lands safely in Stitch's arms, wriggling and shrieking, but Stitch holds her tight to his chest. The flames are getting higher. The floor beneath the balcony is completely consumed by them. He looks up at Gregor.

Stitch can barely see him through the smoke now.

"Gregor!"

Someone grabs Stitch by the shoulder and spins him round. It is Henry.

"We must get away from the house, Stitch!"

"But Gregor!" Stitch turns and points.

The balcony explodes.

Stitch and Henry are knocked off their feet. For a moment, everything is obscured by smoke. Stitch sits up, the girl still in his arms.

The balcony is gone. In its place is a roaring torrent of fire.

"Gregor!" Stitch screams.

But there is no sign of Gregor. Henry drags him and the girl towards the door. Stitch takes one last desperate look back at the flames, then he stumbles out into the night, coughing and spluttering while the girl cries.

He is aware of the relative coolness of the night air and the heat at his back. He sees a ring of people, sweaty and soot-stained, eyes wide, mouths agape.

Stitch lets go of the girl and falls to his knees.

The girl runs to her parents, who embrace her almost as fiercely as Alice now embraces Stitch.

Tears sting Stitch's eyes.

Behind him the house collapses in on itself.

Without Gregor

"He was a good friend, even if only for a short time," says Stitch.

It is early morning. Stitch, Henry and Alice are standing by the smouldering ruin of the house. The people of the village have been tentatively kind to them since their rescue of the family. They've brought them food, which Stitch and Henry can't eat, but Alice accepts their portions with great enthusiasm. The parents of the children they've rescued have thanked them over and over. People have offered them money, new clothes, and yet even in the midst of all this gratitude, Stitch can see the lingering wariness in their eyes.

"It would seem so," says Henry. "He was a very capital fellow. But tell me something Stitch, did he look like us for a particular reason?"

"Yes. He was just like you and me, Henry. The Professor created him."

Henry nudges some pebbles with the toe of his boot, trying his best to look casual. "Oh, oh I see. Which leads me to wonder, and I hope this isn't too much of an impertinence..." He chuckles. "Although the final answer doesn't really mean that much to me, truth be told I don't care either way, what I'm trying to say is..."

"What are you trying to say, Henry?" says Stitch, noting Alice's knowing smile.

Henry squints up at the sky. "Well, where did this fine fellow come along in the scheme of things? When indeed might he have arrived? Not that it matters that much." He shrugs.

"It would seem that he came first, Henry," says Stitch.

Henry is aghast. "This is improbibubble! I came first, Stitch! I'm sure of it!"

Stitch shakes his head.

Henry looks lost. "Are you quite certain?"

Stitch nods.

Henry sighs. "Oh, well, I suppose there are worse things."

"There are," says Stitch, looking mournfully at the ruins of the house.

Someone calls Stitch's name. Stitch and the others turn to find Samuel approaching them, with his daughter and son-in-law supporting him. Both look a little sheepish.

"Stitch, my friend," Samuel calls. "They told me you were here. They told me what you did."

Stitch runs to Samuel. "Samuel, it is so very good to see you."

Samuel embraces Stitch, then holds him at arm's length. "Let me look at you."

Samuel gives his stick to his daughter, then he starts to feel Stitch's face with his hands. Some of the villagers have gathered to watch with fascination.

A beaming smile breaks over Samuel's face. "Yes, you are Stitch. You are most certainly Stitch. My friend."

Stitch watches the village people mutter to each other, some of them looking as if they've seen a miracle. Samuel is delighted to meet Alice again, and Stitch introduces him to Henry. Samuel seems very taken with him. They talk like old friends, but

Stitch notices Alice drift away towards the charred house, her brow furrowed. She has one of her very serious looks. Stitch has learned to gauge the level of seriousness according to the way she arranges her eyebrows and mouth. Going by the way she looks now, this seems very serious indeed. She beckons him towards her.

"Do you know why we didn't find Gregor?" asks Alice.

"The fire was very, very hot, Alice. It disintegrated everything. Even Gregor couldn't have survived."

Alice shakes her head. She takes him round to where the back of the house used to be, where it borders the forest. She points at the ground. Stitch is perplexed by all of this, but he nods when he sees what she's pointing at.

"I see, yes. More ashes."

Alice thumps him playfully on the arm. "No, silly. I don't think Gregor wanted to be found."

Stitch blinks at her in confusion.

"These are tracks," says Alice.

Stitch squints very hard, and truth be told he still doesn't see anything, but his heart starts to flutter.

"You mean?"

Alice smiles. "Gregor is alive."

Not long afterwards, Stitch is leading Henry and Alice into the forest. Stitch has said his goodbyes to Samuel and has promised to return. Samuel has made a point of telling him in front of everyone that he will be "very welcome".

"Where exactly again are we going?" asks Henry.

"We're going to find Gregor," says Stitch. He gestures at Alice. "Well, Alice will be doing most of the finding since she can track."

"Do you really think he's still alive, Stitch?" asks Henry.

"Yes, Alice is certain of it."

Henry looks at the ground. "Alice must have very good eyesight."

"You said Gregor left the castle when the Professor was alive, Stitch," says Alice, "but why do you think he never went away completely if he wasn't happy with what the Professor was doing?"

"Gregor doesn't seem to trust the outside world,

and I suppose it was the only home he'd ever known. It can be difficult to leave one's home completely, I imagine. Although I can only imagine because I have never done it," says Stitch.

"One would have to be the exploring type," says Henry. Now Henry and Alice exchange smiles.

"What?" says Stitch.

"You left the castle, Stitch," says Alice.

Stitch thinks about this. "Yes, I suppose I did."

"You are an explorer, Stitch," says Henry proudly. "Like in *The Great Book of Exploration*. A proper explorer."

He pats Stitch on the back, but Stitch isn't so sure about his comment. He thinks that surely a proper explorer would have gone further, but he keeps this thought to himself.

"I'm sorry I ran away, Stitch," says Henry.

"That's all right, Henry. It was completely 'understandabubble' considering the circumstances."

Henry looks troubled.

"What is it, Henry?"

"I've been thinking since my adventures. Our making, Stitch, the fact that we are…"

"Made from dead things. A philosophical matter that both Alice and I have been discussing. We drew a conclusion."

"Was it a positive one, Stitch?" asks an anxious-looking Henry.

"It was. It is. We are people, Henry. People made from other people, but people just the same."

Henry stops in his tracks and considers this.

"We are people," he says.

"Not just people. The most important type," says Alice.

"What's that now?" asks Henry.

"Good people," says Alice.

They arrive at their final destination in the late afternoon. Stitch is not surprised to find that it is Gregor's cabin. Smoke is coming from the chimney, and the sight of it makes Stitch's heart skip a beat. Seeing where Gregor lives in daylight gives him a better appreciation of the location. Gregor's cabin is small, but from the outside it looks neat and well kept. It is bounded by red and yellow flowers.

The trees behind it lean over it almost protectively, as if conscious that it needs shade.

Stitch goes to the front door and knocks. He feels nervous, especially when there is no reply. He decides to push the door open.

The shades are drawn on the windows, so the only light comes from the small fire burning in the grate. Gregor is sitting bent over by the fire, his hands clasped together. He doesn't turn when Stitch calls his name. Stitch moves closer to him, followed by Henry and Alice.

"Gregor?"

Gregor looks at him. "Stitch," is all he says. He turns back to look at the fire. Stitch looks at his companions; they are as bemused as he is.

"Gregor, why did you leave?"

Gregor wrings his hands together. "Gregor not belong. Gregor stay here."

"But you could have stayed with us," says Stitch.

"Gregor see things. Gregor watch. Gregor always watch. Watch for long time. Watch Small Man waking, watch Stitch waking. Watch world.

Gregor not belong anywhere. Small Man and Stitch not belong either. Gregor better off here. Only place. Best place. Quiet. Alone."

"But what about your friends?" asks Stitch.

Gregor looks stunned. "Friends? Gregor have no friends."

"You have us," says Alice.

Gregor looks at them helplessly. "Friends?"

"Yes, of course. Friends," says Alice.

"You could come back with us to the village, Gregor," says Stitch.

Gregor shakes his head. "No. Gregor not belong in village."

"The village is nice," says Stitch.

"But it's not home," says Alice.

All eyes are on Alice now.

"Then where is home?" asks Henry.

"Wherever friends are," says Alice.

"Friends here?" says Gregor, gesturing around the room.

"No, Gregor, we couldn't," says Stitch. "For one thing this place is too small."

"I can build a house!" shouts Henry.

Stitch is surprised by the outburst. "What's that, Henry?"

"I can build a house." He taps the side of his head. "Part of my hodgepodge bickety bockety brain knows how to do this. It knows all about hammers and wood and nails and saws. It should be easy. I don't just break things: I made a bird house for the Professor once." His face darkens. "Although ... I did accidentally sit on the bird house." His face brightens again. "It's just a matter of making a bigger bird house that we can fit inside."

Henry turns to Stitch and beams proudly. "I must admit, when I set my brain to it, I can be quite smart."

"A big bird house," says Alice, with a raised eyebrow.

"A home," says Stitch.

"Home," says Gregor, slapping his hand on the table and smiling.

A New Home
and an Old Acquaintance

They start building a home, or at least Henry does, mainly with the help of Gregor. The wood and tools arewsupplied by some of the village folk and, as the weeks go by, a house takes shape beside Gregor's cabin.

Sometimes Henry stops in the middle of hammering a nail because he has temporarily forgotten how to hammer. But in moments like that he will usually remember something else from another part of his brain, like how to fish or sow seeds. Alice helps with the building too. She carries and hammers and saws, and Stitch watches in amazement as the house takes shape.

One day Stitch and Henry arrive back from the village after picking up more materials to find a grim-looking Alice standing outside Gregor's door.

"We have a visitor," she says.

Stitch and Henry enter Gregor's house to see a familiar figure waiting for them. Henry gasps. Gregor stands with his arms folded, watching the visitor, as if expecting trouble. The visitor turns to Stitch and smiles. Stitch takes a deep breath.

"Hello again, Professor Hardacre."

Professor Hardacre looks bedraggled. His hair is lank and greasy, and there is a desperate fervent light in his eyes. One hand clutches the locket around his neck. The other grips a sheaf of papers so tightly that they are all scrunched up.

"Well hello there, Stitch. How nice it is to be reacquainted with you after so long. I've heard whispers of your adventures, and I thought to myself I ought to visit my old friend Stitch and see how he's getting on." He looks around the room. "You appear to have found yourself a cosy new home. How delightful."

"Why are you really here, Professor?"

Even Stitch is surprised by the uncompromising tone of his own voice.

Professor Hardacre seems slightly taken aback for a moment, but then he rallies and starts to flatten his papers out on the table with trembling hands.

"I believe we may have got off on the wrong foot," says Professor Hardacre. "But it's all right, I've found a way forward. These old notes of my uncle's point to an exciting new possibility, and I think with your help we can continue his experiments in a new spirit of fellowship and cooperation."

Stitch looks at the others with concern. Alice is shaking her head at Hardacre.

Professor Hardacre gesticulates wildly and projects his voice as if addressing a vast audience. "We must return to first principles. We must take advantage of that one defining component that started my uncle's quest so many years ago."

"And what would that be, Professor?" asks Stitch. The air in the room feels thick and clammy. Henry is muttering "no no no" quietly to himself while rocking back and forth, his eyes fixed on the floor. Alice is breathing hard, her fists balled.

Professor Hardacre straightens up and points at Gregor.

"I require the brute."

Gregor looks confused. A surprised Henry stops his muttering.

"Why?" asks Stitch.

"I'm glad you asked me that question, Stitch," says Hardacre, frantically going through the pages on the table. "It's all in here. I was mistaken when I thought Henry was the first creation, but since you left the castle I came across these notes which my uncle had left to moulder out of sight." He looks contemptuously at Gregor. "Not surprising considering his gross failure. And since our near-mindless friend here was the original creation, it makes perfect sense to use him as the raw material for my future experiments. This time it wouldn't be so much a matter of reconstitution and fusion as much as it will be a matter of dividing the constituent parts and exploring what gave them the vital spark of life."

"You want to take Gregor apart?" Stitch's face feels hot.

Hardacre smirks. "Gregor? You mean you gave it a name? How very droll of you. I can see your reluctance regarding the idea, but just see it from an objective and scientific point of view. Your friend here is little more than raw material to be experimented on, much like your very own White Rabbit."

Stitch glares at Hardacre. "White Rabbit was my friend."

Hardacre guffaws. "A friend, of course. I sometimes forget the importance people ascribe to their pets. Blind sentiment is a powerful force" – he wags a finger – "but scientific rationality is a much more potent—"

"And Gregor is my friend!" says Stitch.

"And mine," says Alice, stepping between the Professor and Gregor.

"And mine too," says Henry, taking his place by Alice's side.

For a moment Hardacre looks at them as if he can't quite believe what he's seeing. Eventually he chuckles. "My, this is very moving indeed. But your loyalty aside you must remember we have great—"

Stitch interrupts. "Great deeds to accomplish, I know, you said that before, Professor. But your great deeds involved changing Henry, and I like Henry just the way he is, and Henry is happy just the way he is, and we like Gregor just the way he is. Gregor is our friend, and Gregor is staying here – with us."

Hardacre's face hardens, his knuckles sharpen to white points as he grips his locket. "Now you listen to me..."

"You wanted to bring them back, didn't you?" says Stitch, nodding at the locket. "Your wife and daughter."

Hardacre's voice is a low hiss, but he suddenly looks very frail, smaller somehow. "How dare you ... how dare you presume to know my intentions!"

Hardacre grins madly. He grabs Stitch by the arm.

"Well then, if I can't have the brute, I can have the next best thing."

He drags Stitch towards the door, but Henry blocks the way.

"I'm sorry, Mr Professor's Nephew. You can't take Stitch. I won't allow it."

Hardacre laughs. "Oh, would like me to hit you again? Is that it? Shall I teach you to know your place?"

Henry looks at him pityingly. This seems to throw Hardacre completely off balance.

"Stop looking at me like that!" he shouts at Henry.

"I can understand why you wanted to bring them back," says Stitch.

Hardacre can't look Stitch or Henry in the eye. He looks around wildly as if seeking a means of escape.

"Stop it. Stop talking about them."

Stitch is undaunted. "Many times I have wanted the Professor back, but I know that's an impossibility. You wanted to bring them back. I think you wanted to do the right thing, but you just went about it the wrong way."

Hardacre throws his head back and screams, "Stop it!"

He lets go of Stitch and grips the locket between both hands, like a drowning man holding on for dear life. His face is contorted in rage as he looks down at Stitch.

"You listen here to me: you are nothing but raw material, and as such you should know your place! You were created by a great man and you should ...

and I will … I will … see to it that his discoveries are put to…"

Professor Hardacre suddenly crumples, as if some terrible weight has settled upon him. He falls to his knees and starts to sob uncontrollably.

"Well now," says Henry quietly, "this is most unexpectalized."

Stitch goes to Professor Hardacre and gently puts a hand on his shoulder.

"Were they good people?" asks Stitch, softly.

"Yes," sniffs Professor Hardacre, unable to look at him.

"The Professor was a good person; he taught me how to be a good person, and Henry also. Perhaps if you think about their good qualities and try to honour them by being good too, then maybe, in some way, they will live through you the way the Professor lives through Henry and me." He looks at Alice. "Alice taught me something too."

"What's that?" asks the Professor, wiping his eyes.

"She taught me that those who leave us are never truly gone, they do go somewhere."

"Where?" asks Professor Hardacre, with a beseeching look.

Stitch lays a hand on his forehead. "They go here." He lays a hand over Professor Hardacre's heart. "And they go here."

Professor Hardacre still looks at him helplessly.

"We live here now, Professor. This is our home, with Gregor. The castle is no place for us any more. We belong out in the world, like everyone else. Thank you for taking the time to visit."

Stitch takes a step back to allow Professor Hardacre to get to his feet. Professor Hardacre silently gathers up his notes. He straightens up and walks towards the door with his head held high. He is stopped in his tracks by Stitch's next words.

"Goodbye, Professor Hardacre. I wish you well."

Professor Hardacre is still for just a moment before he finally leaves through the door. Stitch and the others gather by the door and watch him head in the direction of the village.

"Goodbye, Mr Professor's Nephew," says Henry quietly. "I wish you well also, even with all that transpired before."

Alice pats Henry on the arm.

"I doubt we'll ever see him again," says Alice.

"He go then?" says Gregor.

"Yes, off out into the world," says Stitch.

They watch him disappear out of sight. In that moment Stitch realizes something, and he makes a decision. He turns to his friends.

"I have something to tell you all."

Exploring

Stitch wakes up, just as he always has done for the past eight hundred or so days he has been waking up.

Today is the day. He originally felt bad telling the others about his plan because it clearly made them sad, particularly Henry, but Stitch knows deep down that this is what he needs to do.

He gathers his things in a bag. There are some clothes and a compass given to him by Samuel. He hoists his bag on his back and heads outside to Gregor's house where the others are gathered to meet him, just as arranged. He already feels a tickle of excitement, a sense he is part of something bigger.

"You look like an explorer," says Alice. She smiles a proper smile, and when she hugs him she hugs him fiercely, as he would expect soft Alice to.

Gregor squeezes him. "Good friend, Stitch. Come home soon."

"I will," says Stitch. "And I will have enough stories to write my own book about exploration."

Stitch turns to Henry. Henry doesn't look at him. Instead, he stands sideways, looking up into the sky as if there is something far more interesting up there.

"Well then, Stitch," he says. "I suppose this is goodbye."

"Not goodbye, Henry. I will return soon."

"Well, suit yourself, Stitch. Enjoy the world and all its multifarious sights and sounds and whatnot."

"I will, Henry."

Henry gives a petulant shrug. "Well." Then his lower lip starts to wobble and he turns his back completely on Stitch. Stitch feels terribly guilty, but he knows this is something he simply has to do. He fights the urge to console Henry, knowing to do so might only make things worse.

Stitch waves his friends goodbye, and as he turns to leave he has that feeling of rightness again, because some part of him knows this is what he has always wanted.

He walks on, heading for the village and then the open road. For a long time, all he hears is birdsong and the buzzing of bees. Even though he is happy with his decision, he feels sad when he thinks about Henry. But he almost bursts with joy when he eventually hears someone panting behind him, and the sound of big boots clomping through the grass.

Henry pulls up alongside and falls into step with him. He has a cloth bundle on a stick, which he holds over his shoulder. He continues panting, his tongue sticking out like a dog. He smiles at Stitch.

They walk in silence for a little while, then Henry clears his throat. "You know, you didn't say so Stitch, but knowing you the way I do, and knowing the way my brain works in its mishmashy but rather wise way, I knew it would be best, as did you, that I should accompany you on your travels and your exploralizations."

Stitch stops and looks at Henry. "Do you know something, Henry?"

Henry licks his lips and looks slightly nervous. "I know several somethings, but what specifically, Stitch?" he says.

"I think your mishmashy but rather wise brain was right."

Henry exhales in relief, then puffs out his chest and announces, "Make room world, Stitch and Henry are coming."

He marches on with Stitch. For a moment Stitch looks behind him at the empty castle up on the mountainside. As he turns away from it, he suddenly feels like he's floating, like he can fly. The thought of the boundless possibilities ahead makes him feel light-headed. He looks at the brilliant green of the trees, the soft hazy blue of the mountains.

"Where shall we go, Stitch?"

Stitch smiles. He knows exactly where he wants to go.

"Everywhere," he says.

The End

Acknowledgements

I'd like to thank everyone at Walker Books for their help in introducing Stitch and Henry to the world. Special thanks to Denise Johnstone-Burt and Gráinne Clear for their faith in Stitch's story. Thank you in particular, Gráinne, for your brilliant editorial insight and helping the story to find its feet.

Steve McCarthy provided the wonderful cover and illustrations – thank you, Steve. Big thanks to Maia Fjord for her cover design. Jenny Bish did a brilliant and informative job on the copyedit. Thank you in particular Jenny for "depictorizes", which is one of the most suitably Henryesque words in the book. Thank you, Rebecca J Hall, for a fabulous job on typesetting – the end product made for a very happy Friday indeed. Thank you, Sarah Parker, for your production work. Christine Modafferi swooped in at the end to do an absolutely impeccable proofing job – thank you, Christine.

Special mention as always for Sophie Hicks, simply the best agent ever.

Thank you to the readers, librarians and teachers who have supported my work in so many ways. Huge thanks to the Arts Council of Ireland for supporting my work and for making such a difference to the lives of so many friends and colleagues.

About the Author

Pádraig Kenny is an Irish writer from County Kildare, now living in Limerick. Previously an arts journalist, a teacher and a librarian's assistant, he now writes full-time. His first novel *Tin* and recent *The Monsters of Rookhaven* were both Waterstones Books of the Month. He has twice won the Children's Books Ireland Honour Award for Fiction, has been nominated for the Carnegie Medal and shortlisted for the Irish Book Awards. This is his first book for Walker.

About the Illustrator

Steve McCarthy is an Irish designer and illustrator. His style is bold, colourful and inspired by humour and wit. Steve's first picture book, *The Wilderness*, won the Honour Award for Illustration at the Children's Books Ireland Awards. His poetry anthology with Sarah Webb, *A Sailor Went to Sea, Sea, Sea,* was the 2017 Children's Book of the Year at the Irish Book Awards.

We'd love to hear what you thought of

Stitch

#Stitch
@WalkerBooksUK
@padraig_kenny

Stitch

PÁDRAIG KENNY

WALKER
BOOKS

First published 2024 by Walker Books Ltd
87 Vauxhall Walk, London SE11 5HJ

2 4 6 8 10 9 7 5 3 1

Text © 2024 Pádraig Kenny
Cover and chapter head illustrations © 2024 Steve McCarthy

The author received financial support from
the Arts Council of Ireland in the creation of this work

The right of Pádraig Kenny to be identified as author of this work has been
asserted in accordance with the Copyright, Designs and Patents Act 1988

This book has been typeset in Berkeley Oldstyle

Printed and bound by CPI Group (UK) Ltd, Croydon CR0 4YY

British Library Cataloguing in Publication Data:
a catalogue record for this book is available from the British Library

ISBN 978-1-5295-1778-1

www.walker.co.uk